SONG OF THE SWORD

ANIMAS

C. R. GREY

HOT
KEY
BOOKS

This edition first published in Great Britain in 2016 by
HOT KEY BOOKS
80–81 Wimpole St, London W1G 9RE
www.hotkeybooks.com

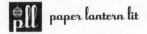

A CIP catalogue record for this book is available from the British Library.

ISBN: 978-1-4714-0133-6
also available as an ebook

1

Printed and bound by Clays Ltd, St Ives Plc

Hot Key Books is an imprint of Bonnier Zaffre Ltd,
a Bonnier Publishing company
www.bonnierpublishing.com

for Aaron, always

Prologue

LITTLE VIVIANA STUMBLED BEHIND the other girls, shielding her eyes with the palm of her hand. The Dust Plains were exactly that—flat plains as far as the eye could see, air thick with dust, a heat so unbearable she swore the sun was just inches away from her skin. But she held her head high, despite the fine powder that lined her mouth and throat.

"I know you're thirsty," one of her captors said. The sound of his voice made her blood boil. When he held out a canteen Viviana's anger overflowed. She swatted it away with the back of her hand and sent it flying. Drops of precious water beaded quickly before disappearing into the cracks of the dry ground. The man glared at her as he reached down to pick it up. When he rose he looked drunk and unsteady, and loomed over Viviana. He lifted his hand, as if to swat her like she did his canteen. Viviana was afraid.

Her bones were shaking. But she stood up taller. She wouldn't give him the satisfaction of cowering.

Another girl stepped between them. Her hair was a dark red, dust matted in her curls.

"She's new," the girl said with a seriousness that belied her years. "She doesn't know how it works yet. But I'll teach her."

The man nodded, almost with respect—even though the girl was the same age as Viviana. "See to it, Annika. Or she's not the only one in for a beating." He walked ahead to oversee the other children. When he was out of earshot the redheaded girl spun around.

"Stupid," she mumbled as she tore away a scrap of her long tunic. "Are you trying to get yourself killed?"

"I'm not a slave," Viviana said. It was the first words she'd spoken since she'd been captured. "I won't act like one."

"I suppose you're from the Gray," Annika said, mimicking Viviana's accent. "Well, guess what?" She pointed at the line of girls who walked ahead. The scrap of her tunic fluttered in the wind. "The rest of us *are* slaves. And if you think you're better than us—"

"I don't think that," Viviana said quickly. "Not for a second." A sense of shame bloomed in her chest. Her father, King Melore, always said they were not above the people they served.

"Then act like it. Walk with the rest of us, do as we do. The only way to survive is to work together." Annika held out the scrap of fabric. "Tie this around your head to cover your mouth and nose. We'll go see if any of the other girls have a sip of water to share."

"Thank you," Viviana said after she'd tied the muslin around her face.

"Thank me by staying alive," Annika said gruffly, as if she were an old soul in a girl's body.

Viviana followed Annika silently as they caught up with the rest of the camp. Viviana realized it was the first kindness anyone had shown her since leaving the Gray, and she wouldn't soon forget it. But she didn't agree that they were slaves. If she escaped—no, *when* she escaped—she'd remember that every person should be free.

One

VIVIANA STOOD TALL OVER Bailey; her violet eyes flashed as though lit from within by strikes of cold lightning.

"You die today, Child of War," she said. Bailey felt her fingers grasp his throat. Her nails dug into his skin. "You cannot defeat me—I can control whatever I wish. Even life itself."

Bailey tried to speak, to tell her that she was wrong, that the bond would always triumph over Dominance, but her hands were fast around his neck. He couldn't breathe. He grabbed her wrists to pull them away, but suddenly she was gone, and in her place was the Jackal.

"We had a deal, boy," he hissed. His hands were just as strong, just as angry, as Viviana's.

"No . . ." Bailey said, just barely audible above the noise of bird screech and dog howl surrounding him. The Jackal grinned.

"Bailey, wake up!" The Jackal's voiced had changed—he sounded almost like Hal. "Wake up, Bailey, you're dreaming!"

Bailey opened his eyes. Hal's face hovered above him. Bailey lay on his back on a cold dirt floor, cocooned in a wool blanket.

"It's just a dream," Hal said. "The Fair is over. You're in the tunnels."

Bailey blinked his eyes, and all of a sudden, his vision was overtaken by a mess of white fur and a giant, wet tongue. Taleth planted a long, loving lick on the side of Bailey's face.

"*Oof!* Yuck!" Bailey laughed. "I'm awake, I'm awake!" The tiger purred and settled back onto her haunches.

"Still having those nightmares about the Fair?" Hal asked. He sat hugging his own blanket around his knees.

"Yeah," said Bailey. "I know the Jackal's dead, but..."

"I know," said Hal. "I think about it a lot too. And it's not as though we're safe from the Dominae. Not even here."

"Here" was a place that Bailey had never even known existed until after the Reckoning—and it was practically in his old backyard. Along with Tremelo and the allied RATS and Velyn, Bailey and his friends had spent the last two weeks hiding out in a series of crisscrossing underground tunnels that stretched all the way from the Fluvian River in the west, south through the Lowlands, and into the Dark Woods.

Tremelo had been the one to lead them there. After their escape from the Gray City, Tremelo had brought the tired band of fighters to a cave entrance, and stood back as, one by one, the fighters entered and gaped at the seemingly endless pathway before them. Bailey had stood close to Tremelo and had noticed a pain behind his teacher's eyes as he watched the others enter the tunnel.

"What's wrong?" he'd asked.

"The Jackal engineered these tunnels," Tremelo said. "His soldiers used them to ambush the Velyn. I hate to bring Eneas and his people down here, to make them relive that terror, but these passageways are undeniably the easiest way into the Woods without being seen."

Bailey had shuddered at the mention of the Jackal's name. Before that spring, he'd already known that the Jackal had massacred the Velyn and murdered Tremelo's mentor, the Loon. But his own recent ordeal at the Jackal's hands had made Bailey eager never to think about him again. He would have killed me, he thought. He almost did.

Despite their sinister origins, the tunnels proved to be an excellent hiding place, although the threat of the Dominae still hung in the air. Everywhere Bailey went in the underground tunnels, he imagined Viviana and her soldiers standing directly above him, armed and ready for him to show his face in the sunlight. He hadn't been sleeping much, and when he did, Viviana and the Jackal were always waiting for him in his dreams.

"Did I wake you up?" he asked Hal.

"Me? No," Hal answered. "I've been awake for hours."

Bailey heard the unmistakable sound of bats careening through the next tunnel. Someone shouted, undoubtedly someone who did not appreciate being woken by their squeaks. Hal smiled.

"It doesn't help that this ground is hard as a rock," Bailey said. "What I wouldn't give for a real bed." It had been many weeks since Bailey and Hal had fled Fairmount in pursuit of Taleth and her kidnappers. In that time, they'd slept on the rigimotive and a North River barge, in an abandoned warehouse, and on the cold stone floor of the Jackal's prison. All Bailey wanted was some normal rest. But the world that he'd once considered normal now seemed like a place he hadn't visited in years.

"I was just thinking of going to the workshop," Hal said to Bailey. "Knowing our king's irregular sleep patterns, I figured I'd find him there and see if I could help out with his project."

Bailey pulled his blanket off and sat up.

"I don't really want to go back to sleep," he said, his nightmare still lingering in his mind. "I'll come too."

A burst of bats overhead greeted them as they left their small sleeping nook and entered the high-ceilinged tunnel that led to Tremelo's makeshift workshop. Here, the tunnels were wide enough that Taleth padded behind them with room to move freely, though they narrowed toward the Lowlands, cramped and damp, and smelling strongly of moss. Light from dynamo lamps and small campfires reflected warmly on the tunnel walls, guiding Bailey and Hal past huddled groups of allied fighters, some of whom were snoring under their blankets, and some of whom were awake and whispering about what might be going on in the kingdom above them. A hush fell over the fighters as they passed, a look of awe and curiosity in their eyes. Taleth had that affect on people.

The tunnel curved; up ahead, a wash of bright torchlight illuminated the entrance to a wide cavern. Inside, Tremelo—the True King of Aldermere—crouched over a wobbly table.

His back was to the boys as they entered the cavern. Hearing their footsteps, he turned to look over his shoulder at them.

"It's late; what are you two doing awake?" he asked.

"Couldn't sleep," said Bailey. "We thought maybe you'd want some help."

"I'll settle for company," Tremelo said. Pushed to the side of the table were the remains of the Halcyon machine, which had helped them overcome Viviana's Dominance that terrible day at the Fair. Its inner nest of wires had been exposed and pulled out, and the orb that had once sat in its center was in pieces, like silver bits of eggshell, on the table in front of Tremelo.

"Look at this," Tremelo said. "I think I've finally solved it."

Fennel the fox entered; Tremelo lifted her from the floor to the table and gave her an affectionate scratch behind her ear. Her leg, which had been injured in the Reckoning, had not healed perfectly, and she could not move as spryly as she had before.

"I've been thinking of the next phase of the Halcyon all wrong," Tremelo said. Bailey heard a familiar lilt in Tremelo's voice—no matter how regal Tremelo's new title made him, he was a true tinkerer at heart, always the most excited when surrounded by scraps of metal. "Since the Fair, I've agonized over how to make the Halcyon bigger, in order to magnify the healing effects of the bond even more. Big enough to protect an entire army against Dominance! But *bigger* isn't the answer at all!"

He held up two identical objects for Bailey and Hal to see. They were the size and shape of robins' eggs, patchworked together from bits of the original metal orb, each dangling from a piece of twine long enough to hang around a person's neck.

"Here, take them," Tremelo said, pushing the objects at Bailey and Hal. The metal was cool in Bailey's palm.

"These amulets are the perfect answer to Viviana's technology," Tremelo said. "Instead of projecting the bond's energy from one central orb, we could create enough of these to supply our fighters with their own strengthening power. And it doesn't just protect them alone—no, just watch!"

Grinning, Tremelo reached for a third amulet and then faced Hal and Bailey.

"Concentrate on your kin," he instructed them. "Tap into the bond."

Bailey glanced at Taleth, who'd laid down on her stomach, her paws extended and her head alert. Her tail batted against the dusty ground. He'd never felt so much a part of the world than he had since his Awakening. He knew that as long as he had Taleth, he'd never feel alone.

The metal amulet grew warmer; Bailey felt himself falling into Taleth's mind. He watched himself and Hal and Tremelo standing by the work table. He felt his tail—Taleth's tail—beating lazily on the floor. His whiskers twitched in amusement. Then his view shifted again: he was no longer Taleth, but he wasn't Bailey, either. For a split second, he felt himself flying, fluttering, darting just below the dirt ceiling of the tunnels. It was exhilarating! He heard his companions squeaking, beckoning him to follow. And finally, he saw himself, Hal, and Tremelo again—but this time, from the worktable. Looking down, he saw reddish-black paws and a fluffy, swishing tail. One of those paws still throbbed with pain; a bone had not set correctly.

"Isn't it marvelous?" said Tremelo. Bailey stepped back, almost tripping over his own feet.

"How did we do that?" he asked. "I was inside Fennel's mind—and a bat's, too!"

"That was impossible," said Hal. "Wasn't it?"

"We triangulated!" said Tremelo, beaming with excitement. "I suspect the more people you were to try it with, the less intense it would be. But just think of the possibilities! Just as Viviana used her orb to strengthen her Dominance, we strengthened each other's bonds! Even if we never achieved that level of intensity on the battlefield—to give each fighter their own tool to counter Dominance—it could be the key to defeating Viviana!"

"How can we make enough, though?" Hal asked. "This metal is precious, isn't it?"

Tremelo's energy deflated like a ripped rigimotive dirigible.

"I haven't quite figured that part out yet," he said. "Though at the rate we're gathering fighters, it may not matter. We barely have enough Allies to take on a fraction of Viviana's army."

Just then, a long howl echoed through the tunnels, followed by several shrieks. Bailey thought he heard Eneas Fourclaw, the leader of the Velyn, shouting commands.

"Are we being attacked?" Bailey whispered. His heart began to pound. Taleth leapt up onto all fours and faced the entrance to the workspace.

"Stay close," said Tremelo. He took up a crossbow that leaned against the wall and stepped cautiously out into the tunnel.

The tunnel had become crowded with RATS and Velyn anxious to know what had happened. Tremelo and the boys were met by Eneas Fourclaw, who walked toward them with his hands raised.

"It's all right," Eneas said. "No need to panic. One of our wolves attacked a RAT ally's deer kin. People are a little upset, but it's nothing to get up in arms about."

"A kill?" asked Tremelo. "Inside the tunnel?"

Eneas shrugged.

"People are getting restless, and their kin along with them," the warrior said. "We've been trying to send the animals outside to hunt, but what more can we do? I can't curb every predator's instincts. We're all cooped up in here. Things get out of hand."

Bailey saw a flash of bright-red hair belonging to Gwen. Beside her were Phi and Tori; Phi waved at them. Bailey grabbed Hal's sleeve and together they crept along the wall, away from Tremelo's and Eneas's raised voices, to join the girls.

"Everyone having a pleasant morning so far?" asked Tori, with a knife's sharpened edge to her voice. "I know I could have used more sleep.... What's that?" She pointed at Bailey's hand, and he realized that he still held Tremelo's amulet in his closed fist.

"Tremelo was showing them to us," he explained. When he reached the part about seeing not only through Taleth's eyes, but through the eyes of Tremelo's and Hal's kin as well, he noticed that Gwen looked away sharply.

"What's wrong?" he asked.

"Nothing," said Gwen. "I'm glad it worked for you, that's all."

Phi moved closer to Gwen so that their shoulders were touching, her brown eyes full of sympathy.

"What do you mean?" Hal asked. "Why wouldn't it?"

"Hal..." said Phi in a way that urged him to let it drop.

"No, it's all right," Gwen said. "There's no point in being coy about it. I was in the workshop yesterday evening, when Tremelo had finished building the first two. He let me try it ... and I didn't feel anything. Not like I expected to, I guess."

"What do you mean?" Bailey asked. He found it difficult to believe that Gwen had lost faith in Tremelo's tinkering. "You don't think he can get it to work?"

Gwen looked down at the floor for a moment, and then took a deep breath before speaking again. "I don't know if he can get it to work for *me*. I haven't felt the bond at all since we left the Gray City. Ever since I nearly . . ." She paused. "I almost killed one of my own kin, and I think that it . . . I don't know, that it *severed* something. My kin haven't come near me since."

"Dominance did this," said Phi, placing her hand on Gwen's shoulder. "Probably lots of people at the Fair that day are having the same trouble. But I'm sure it'll get better. That your bond will—"

"I know that it's not just me." Gwen gave Phi a sad smile and shrugged. "It doesn't make it any easier, though." She looked like she might cry in front of all of them.

Just then a small group of adults entered at the far end of the tunnels. It looked like a small procession, all of them huddled around a RAT woman and offering her comfort. She had her hands up to her face, her shoulders shaking, as she was being led back to her camp. Bailey could tell it was her deer kin that had been killed.

Bailey turned his attention back to Gwen. "Your bond will come back," he said, wanting to make it all right. "It lives inside us. Viviana can't change that."

"I want to believe that," Gwen said. "But right now I feel like there's a hole in my chest that used to be full of feeling. You've only just Awakened—can't you imagine how you would feel if suddenly your bond with Taleth was taken away?"

Bailey could, and the thought made him shudder.

All day, Bailey carried the worry of what Gwen had told him. He watched his fellow Allies carefully during a communal dinner of thistle-and-root stew, looking for the same sadness in their eyes that he'd seen in Gwen's. But he couldn't tell whether the fighters in the tunnel were suffering from a weakened bond, or simply from their cramped and anxious habitat. He knew that if Gwen was right, defeating Viviana and the Dominae would be even harder. Without their bonds, the Allies would need more than just Tremelo's tinkered amulets.

He left the hushed whispers and flickering firelight of the tunnels and walked out into the twilight for some air. He wasn't alone: Eneas Fourclaw sat on the wide, flat rock that the Allies used to keep watch over the tunnel entrance. Eneas pointed over Bailey's shoulder.

"Your shadow's looking well," he said.

Bailey turned. Taleth stood behind him. Her whiskers shook as she sniffed the night air.

"She's happy to be outside," said Bailey.

"I believe that," Eneas said. "She's handling the tunnels well, though." Bailey heard the unspoken thought behind Eneas's words: Taleth was remaining calm, unlike some others.

"That woman whose kin was killed today—will she be all right?" Bailey asked.

Eneas swept a crawling beetling off of his thigh.

"Kin die all the time," he said. "You're not used to how it works yet, are you?"

"How what works?" Bailey asked.

"Being a predator," Eneas answered. He nodded to his kin, the mountain lion Elspeth, who lay on her side next to him on the rock. "Lions, bears, wolves—they have to hunt and kill to survive. Can be hard to wrap your mind around it, once you become one."

"*I'm* not a predator," said Bailey.

Eneas smiled. His blue eyes were kind, even though his skin was rough from many years living in the elements of the Peaks.

"But *she* is," he said, gesturing to Taleth. "And that means you've got something of that in you too. Only natural."

Bailey felt a little ill. He remembered the Jackal's cry as his own dog had attacked him at the Progress Fair, and the limp body of Joan Sucrette. But Bailey hadn't been the one to kill them.

"Don't look so frightened at the thought," Eneas said. "As Velyn, we know that our kin will do one another harm—we acknowledge it as best we can. Doesn't make you any less human. More, maybe."

Eneas rose from the rock; Elspeth stretched and stood as well.

"My watch is over," he said. "You wouldn't mind going in to find my replacement, would you?"

"I'll take the watch," Bailey said. He wasn't quite ready to trade the peacefulness of the dusky forest for the stifling air in the tunnels. "If that's all right with you."

Eneas tugged at his blond beard. He looked from Bailey to Taleth, who flicked her whiskers eagerly.

"I suppose you're ready," he said. "Besides, your beast Taleth is the best protection any watchman could hope for. I'll let Tremelo know."

Eneas ducked into the tunnel, but Bailey was aware of the large green eyes of Elspeth the mountain lion, watching over him from the entrance.

"Not *quite* ready to do it alone, I guess." Bailey sighed. He pushed himself up onto the rock and took a deep, invigorating breath of the fresh night air. From here, he could see the bank of the pine-covered hillside, dipping down toward the edge of a cliff that overlooked the river. If anyone were to try and enter the tunnels from here, they'd be spotted nearly half a mile away.

As he always did when he looked north toward the Lowlands, he thought of his mom and dad. They were down there somewhere, past the dark ribbon of the river, on the other side of the wide stretch of trees whose shadowy branches could hide any number of threats. He wished he could make the journey to see them, but Tremelo had forbidden it. Ever since they'd arrived at the tunnels, and Bailey realized how close they were to the Lowlands, he'd found himself missing his mom and dad more than ever. He wanted to sit at the dinner table over thick, crusty bread and a bowl of corn porridge and tell them everything—about his Awakening, about the prophecy that had entangled him with the fate of the kingdom, about his friends.

Somewhere in the silent pines, a twig snapped.

Taleth jumped to her feet, her whiskers and tail twitching. The skin on Bailey's arms prickled under his sweater and coat. He was sure that someone was watching them.

A crackle; a rustle—something moved in the trees just downhill from them. Bailey peered into the dark and saw a figure moving away from them quickly. His heart pounded. He leapt up. For a frenzied moment, he was unsure what to do. He looked back at Elspeth, but she was gone. He knew he couldn't let the stranger get away. Together, he and Taleth left their post and rushed down the hill. Just ahead, he saw the silhouette of the running spy. They darted between trees and into deeper shadows until it was nearly impossible for Bailey to see what it was he was following. Taleth rushed ahead, and Bailey relied on her vision and smell to lead him.

They sped around trees and over rocks. Ahead, Bailey could barely make out the running figure. Then the person—a man, Bailey guessed—made a sharp turn, nearly slipping on some moss. He skidded down a small hill. Just ahead, a beam of light shone from behind an outcrop of rocks, and Bailey froze. The man was not alone. Bailey's heart had already been beating loudly from the pursuit, but now it pulsed in his chest like the tightly drawn skin of a drum.

Taleth lunged ahead, growling, and disappeared behind the rocks.

"Quindley! Quindley!" shouted a voice quavering with fear. Taleth reappeared, dragging a man by his coat. "Oh, dear merciful Nature!" the man cried.

"Coming!" called a second voice, and the light beam shifted. A portly figure followed Taleth out from behind the rocks, holding a dynamo lamp. The lamplight hit Bailey right in the eyes, and he put up his hands to shield them from the glow.

"Good grief, it's Bailey," said the portly figure. "Miller, you fool, get up!"

The light swung away, and Bailey moved his hands. The rotund man standing before him, in a long brown coat with many bulging pockets, was none other than Hal's uncle, Roger Quindley.

"Preserve me!" shouted the man whom Taleth now had pinned to the mossy ground. "Save me!"

"Bailey, call her off, will you?" Roger asked. "He's a friend."

"Taleth, stop," Bailey said, but Taleth had already read his thoughts. She backed away from the man and sat down on her haunches.

The man pulled himself up from the ground. He had a patchy reddish-brown beard and wore a traveling cloak with a wide collar, and a leather satchel swung over his shoulder—this was no fighter. The beady eyes of two frightened weasels peered out from inside the cloak.

"Ants alive, boy, you ought to know better than to frighten people like that," said Roger.

"What in Nature?!" exclaimed the stranger. He stared at Taleth. "I had heard, but I didn't believe—it's *true*. A white tiger, after all these years!"

"Her name is Taleth," said Bailey warily.

"I saw her through the trees, and at first glance I thought she was a ghost!" the man said. "Roger, you could have warned me!"

"Bailey, you look very unwell. When was the last time you slept?" Roger asked.

"Who is this?" Bailey asked, ignoring Roger's question.

"Ah, yes," said Roger. "This is Mr. Miller, and he's come a long way to meet with Tremelo. This," he continued, pointing to Bailey, "is Bailey Walker."

Mr. Miller ran a hand through his mussed hair. One of the weasels that had been hiding in his coat emerged onto the ground and skittered onto a rock. "So you must be the same young man who challenged Viviana in the Gray City? You must be—your Animas is unmistakable!"

"You've heard of me?" asked Bailey.

"I come from a small town in the northwestern peaks," said the man. "But even there, word has spread. You and that man who was with you—the one claiming to be Trent Melore—you're the most wanted persons in Aldermere. Every village between the Gray and the Lowlands is filled with Dominae officers, trying to find you! It's an honor, I must say, and a relief, to see you still safe."

Roger frowned. At his feet, a bulky, round badger waddled about, sniffing at the ground. The badger, Dillweed, seemed completely unimpressed by Taleth, who watched his every movement.

"You're not alone, are you, Bailey?" asked Roger. "You have protection, aside from your kin?"

Bailey opened his mouth to answer, but he didn't have to.

"Bailey!"

He heard Tremelo's voice behind him in the distance. Suddenly, they were surrounded—Tremelo, Eneas, Elspeth, Digby Barnes, and Hal burst through the trees, followed by a handful of RAT and Velyn fighters. Tremelo grabbed Bailey's shoulder.

"You and Taleth were supposed to be keeping watch," he said.

"We were," said Bailey. "We saw someone sneaking around, and followed them here—"

"You shouldn't have left the tunnel!" Tremelo argued. "You should have woken someone else. Instead, by leaving no one at the watch, you left us open to attack!"

Bailey felt his stomach drop. It was clear Tremelo didn't think him ready for the responsibility. He looked to Eneas for support, but Eneas frowned, his eyes stony.

"*Think* before you run off, boy," Tremelo said. He shook his head. "You never *think*. If Elspeth hadn't come to fetch us—"

"Of course I *think*!" yelled Bailey. "*I* was the one who found Taleth when she was kidnapped, and who stood up to Viviana at the Fair. *I* sent you the Clamoribus, or you'd have never raised an army to fight! *You've* barely done—"

"Everything *you've* done has been the direct result of leading with your instincts, which are practically wild," said Tremelo, his voice calm but still steely. "You run away from safety and rush into battle, ignoring obvious danger. The entire kingdom is on the brink of war. Now is the time for calculation, not rashness!"

"Please, please," said Roger, stepping between Tremelo and Bailey. He puffed up his chest and jerked his shoulders back, causing a sprig of fresh herbs to fall out of his front coat pocket. "There's no harm done—he made a very intimidating watchman, I must say! Scared poor Mr. Miller out of his skin."

"And who is 'Mr. Miller'?" asked Eneas. "I've warned you before about exposing us, Quindley...."

"Please, calm down!" Roger huffed. "Of course you can trust me! This man has some information, and if he hadn't come to me, he'd have been wandering the Dark Woods for days looking for you all. And then where would you be?"

"You could have been followed!" Eneas shouted.

Digby Barnes stepped between them.

"Eneas, my friend," he said. "Roger means well. And without his help—"

"We don't need some meddling worm-head marking the path straight to our door," Eneas said.

Tremelo addressed Mr. Miller. "What information do you bring?" he asked.

Miller looked from Tremelo to Eneas and Digby, and back to Roger.

"Tell them what you told me, Miller," said Roger.

Mr. Miller nodded, swallowed, then began his report.

"I come with news from Everglen, near the Seers' Valley," he said. "It's a peaceful place—we'd heard of the Dominae there, but hadn't had any dealings with them until a few weeks ago."

The fighters had created a circle around the man; his two weasels stood alert and wary of the many eyes that watched their human kin.

"My fellow townsfolk and I began to notice more Dominae soldiers in the village, and many of us sensed from our kin that a disturbance was growing in the forest. We sent a party to investigate, and found a Dominae camp in the peaks just west of Seers' Valley. They've been busy carving into the mountain, creating some sort of mine. I had to tell someone, so I journeyed to the city to find the resistance groups. Their trail led me to a small group of loyalists living in the sewers underneath the Gudgeons. They told me to come here. I met Roger in the village just north of here, and he agreed to bring me."

"Just like that, eh?" Eneas said to Roger. "No thought to the consequences of bringing a stranger into these woods?"

"Can you tell us what the Dominae is mining?" asked Tremelo.

"I can't rightly say what it's called," said Miller. "But the stone is black and smooth as coal and sends up a powerful ash. It's covering half the valley—and their hammering away at it rings over the peaks."

Bailey watched as Eneas's face turned to stone. He stepped back and looked out at the trees, as though expecting something menacing to come charging out from the shadows.

"They're building something with this material?" Tremelo asked.

Miller nodded his head.

"I didn't get a very good look at these contraptions," he said. "But they're larger than men, and there are a great many of them."

A frightened hush settled over the gathered Allies. Bailey reached out to Taleth, to feel the comfort of her soft fur. He knew all too well how crafty Viviana and her tinkerers could be.

"Thank you," said Tremelo. He shook Mr. Miller's hand. "Do you need lodging? Conditions in the tunnels aren't spectacular, but we could find a spot for you."

Miller waved his hand to decline.

"I have cousins in the Dust Plains," he said. "I'm headed northeast to warn them. Dark times, sir. Dark times."

Miller nodded a curt good-bye to Eneas and Digby, and, to Bailey's surprise, stopped to cautiously pet Taleth before heading into the trees. As soon as Miller's back was to them, Eneas called to a young Velyn fighter.

"Follow him," he told the man. "Just to make sure he won't run straight to the Dominae."

"Is that necessary?" asked Roger, annoyed.

"We can't be too careful," said Eneas.

"If you insist," huffed Roger. "But if you trust *me*, you can trust Miller."

"I *don't* trust you," Eneas replied.

"All right," said Tremelo, interrupting them. "Roger, will you escort Mr. Miller to the nearest village? And keep watch on him."

"Fine, fine," Roger said.

Tremelo pulled Eneas toward the trees, where they began to speak together in the low voices that Bailey understood to be heavy laden with war talk. Roger approached him and Hal.

"And how are my boys?" Roger asked. He placed an arm around Hal's shoulders and gave him a comforting squeeze. "My nephew, the revolutionary! Never been prouder." Dillweed the badger looked up at Taleth and sneezed unappreciatively.

"We're all right," said Bailey. "Sorry I scared your friend earlier."

"Do you believe Mr. Miller about the mines, Uncle Roger?" Hal asked.

"No reason not to," he replied. "There's plenty of mischief that's been going on out there since Viviana's 'Fair.' Wouldn't surprise me a bit." Roger patted Taleth's head. "You boys have everything you need here, don't you? You let me know if there's anything I can do." He gave Hal a squeeze on the shoulder before leaving, then immediately came back and hugged his nephew so hard Hal's eyes looked like they might pop out of his head. "Be careful," he added. Then he patted all of his bulging coat pockets to make sure everything was in order before he left a second time. He turned to follow Miller down the path. Bailey hastened after him.

"There is something you can do for me," Bailey said, catching up.

"Ah, of course!" said Roger. He stopped. "I almost forgot—they're well and safe." He meant Herman and Emily Walker, Bailey's mom and dad. "There's been a great deal of Dominae soldiers passing through the village," Roger continued. "And I did worry when I saw they were no longer at their farm...."

"What?" Bailey interrupted. "Where are they?"

"With a neighbor," said Roger. "Apparently, the Dominae came to question them. They got scared to be in the house with just the two of them. Too exposed."

Bailey's chest ached at the thought of his mom and dad frightened out of their once-peaceful home. Worse, they didn't even know why.

"Don't worry, Bailey," Roger said. "They're safe for now, and I haven't told them a thing about your Awakening or where you are. When the Dominae ask, they won't be lying by saying they know nothing. They're right worried, though. Sometimes I wish I didn't know, either; it breaks my heart to see them hurting so."

"Thanks," said Bailey, his own heart even heavier than it had been just a few moments before.

"Better catch up with Miller," said Roger. "Be safe!" He set off into the trees. Dillweed waddled after him.

Near the tunnel, Tremelo and Eneas's low-voiced talk had grown into an argument.

"We need more than just tinkering on our side!" Eneas was saying. "We need a real army!"

"I agree," said Tremelo. "I've always agreed, but how are we to protect that army once we've acquired it? I can't abandon this experiment. Not when you yourself have admitted that there's been a change in the bond!"

"I've told you where to look—"

"Eneas, I won't risk the safety of this camp on a fairy story!" said Tremelo. "We need to find another way. . . . Digby!" He called to Digby Barnes, the red-faced leader of the Gray City RATS. "Surely we can reach out to those RATS who are still in hiding."

Eneas paced. "We can't fight the Dominae with a pack of old men!" he shouted.

"I beg your pardon!" said Digby. "I'm only fifty-four!"

"Eneas, be reasonable," said Tremelo. "Calm down; let's go inside. We're just courting trouble, yelling in the woods like this."

He patted Digby's shoulder, urging him into the tunnel. Eneas stormed past with Elspeth at his heels. Then Tremelo fixed his eyes on Bailey. He sighed.

"I'm sorry I spoke so harshly before," he said. "I was worried. Anything could have happened to you."

"You didn't have to worry," said Bailey. "I had Taleth with me—and besides, that's what you're supposed to do when you're on watch, isn't it? I saw someone in the woods; I wanted to make sure they weren't going to hurt us."

Tremelo stroked his mustache, which had recently joined forces with a full beard. "Just take care of yourself."

"Fine," Bailey mumbled. Why did everyone assume that he *couldn't*? He'd been through so much already, and was still alive. "Why was Eneas so upset?" he asked.

Tremelo's shoulders slumped; Bailey noticed shadows under his eyes.

"It doesn't matter," Tremelo answered. "Everyone has different ideas about what to do next, that's all. And if Mr. Miller's report is to be trusted, then we're up against an unknown."

"What do we do?" Bailey asked.

Tremelo smiled wearily.

"We keep hoping," he said. He gripped Bailey's shoulder. "Get some sleep tonight, all right? I'll send one of Digby's men out on the watch."

As he lay awake under his coat that night, Bailey turned the encounter with Mr. Miller over in his mind. Miller had been relieved and honored, as he put it, to see Bailey alive. Bailey wondered just what the people in Aldermere who lived farther from the City, the people like his mom and dad in the Golden Lowlands, knew about the Dominae, and about him. The Child of War. Had his and Taleth's appearance at the Fair only served to start a whirl of rumors, or were there people out there who actually had hope that a True King lived, and that the prophecy was real and coming true? Those were the people he and the Allies needed to find, he knew. But the kingdom was scattered with spies, and he hardly knew where to start.

Bailey awoke the next morning when Taleth, who had been snoring at his side, suddenly leapt up onto all fours and bared her teeth.

"What's going on?" he asked as her lashing tail nearly hit him in the forehead. Four Velyn men ran past his niche with their weapons in their hands.

"He took his knives, his bow—even his extra boots," one of them was saying.

"He's coming back, isn't he?" said another.

Bailey rose from his blanket on the floor and followed Taleth out into the tunnel. All along the passageway, nervous Velyn men and women clumped together, whispering.

"He wouldn't just leave us like this," said a healer woman, pulling her shawl tightly around her shoulders. "Does he want us to leave too?"

"I thought he trusted Tremelo," said the young fighter she was speaking to. He flexed the claws affixed to his right hand. "Perhaps he didn't, after all. Perhaps none of us should."

Bailey looked away and hurried to Tremelo's workshop. There he found Tremelo speaking with Gwen and Digby.

"What's going on?" he asked.

Tremelo stood stroking his mustache; his brow was lined with worry.

"It's Eneas," he said. "He's disappeared."

Two

"HOW CAN WE BE certain that the other Velyn won't up and leave as well?"

"Did he say anything to anyone about where he's gone?"

"We can't wait any longer to reach out to the other RATS! We need more of our *own* people on our side!"

The shouts of the men inside Tremelo's workspace reminded Gwen of her days as the Elder's apprentice, sitting in on countless debates and speeches, taking notes as one red-faced, fist-shaking dignitary after the next laid out their opinions and plans. She and her friends leaned against the cavern wall and watched as the RATS argued among themselves. Bailey seemed anxious to join in the war talk, though Gwen suspected that the seasoned warriors and revolutionaries in the room would not be pleased to hear from a schoolboy. As for her, she was content to stay quiet. Her mind felt cloudy.

At times like this she would've played her harmonica, but when she rode in Tremelo's motorbuggy through the deranged crowd of kin at the Progress Fair, her owls had attacked her—and she'd lost it then.

"Already there's rumors going round the tunnels that Eneas never trusted you," said Merrit, an Animas Sheepdog who had been with the RATS since the days of the Loon, Tremelo's mentor. "Even if it's not true—even if he was taken, or something like that—the damage has been done. The Velyn will start to leave if we don't take action now!"

"And what kind of action is that?" Tremelo asked. "We don't have the forces to march against Viviana, and we risk opening ourselves to attack if we begin recruiting among normal citizens. We need to remain strong, and reach out to those whom we know will join us. We can't be taking risks!"

Digby Barnes swept his red knit cap from his head and used it to wipe his brow.

"It's going to be a hard task, tracking down what RATS is in hiding," he said. "You all know the Dominae's been hunting down RATS Nests. Why, even on the journey here from the Gray City, the Dominae was behind us, and probably figured Bailey here would stop in the first RATS Nest he could find. I know I'll never forget seein' the meeting place of the Arden RATS set alight from the top of that hill. We ken only hope they all made it out alive, and even if we do find them, they's only five men and women strong." He shook his head, his eyes narrow and grim.

"But there must be others out there who would fight on our side," said Bailey. As Gwen had expected, the RATS all looked at him with mild annoyance. "Nearly everyone in the kingdom saw or heard of what Viviana did at the Fair! They know she's evil!"

"It's not as easy as knowing what's right and what's wrong," said Tremelo. "Fear is a terrible hindrance. And in that regard, Viviana got exactly what she wanted on the Equinox—she made everyone in Aldermere fear her."

"And she scattered our kind to the four corners as well," spat Digby. "I'll do what I can, with Roger's help, but I make no guarantees."

"We have to try," said Tremelo. "I leave it to you, my friend, to use every resource you can to find us more allies. As for me . . ."

"Ever the tinkerer," said Merrit.

"Yes, that's right," said Tremelo. "Eneas didn't understand, and I don't expect all of you to, either. But the Dominae is too powerful to defeat with manpower alone. I will stay here and continue my experiments in the hope that I may be able to protect us from Viviana when we are finally ready to face her."

"Protect us?" said Merrit. "We don't want to be protected from Dominance; we want to *destroy* Dominance! How do you propose we do that? With your little trinkets?"

"Easy," Digby said as he crossed his arms. "That's the king you're talking to."

"Well, I knew him as the Loon's boy before he was ever a king," Merrit shot back. "Tremelo, I'm sorry if you need to grow a thicker skin, but here and now we need solutions—"

Gwen breathed in deeply; all this talk of fighting, of war, made her feel queasy. She'd already lost her dearest friend, the Elder. How many more of her friends would she lose to Viviana's rage?

She sat down with her back against the cavern wall. Her head swam, and her vision clouded. She held her hands up to her eyes. Not now. She didn't want a vision to happen now, in front of all of these people. Not many knew of her newly discovered gift. If her status as a Seer became widely known, she would be pulled in all directions by Allies wanting to know how best to proceed. But she couldn't stop the light from growing.

Your Glass is calling to you, my dear, sang a voice in Gwen's memory—Ama, the Seer whom she'd met before Viviana's Fair. *You can feel it beckoning to you.*

She peeled back the flap of her rucksack. Indeed, the interior of the bag was lit by a slightly pulsing, pearlescent glow. As she reached in and cupped it with both hands, she marveled at how beautiful it was—ribbons of light, like sun on a moving stream, rippled through its angles and planes. Instinctively, she stepped back, away from the group—and the voices in the tunnel began to fade away. The light behind her eyes scrubbed away everything in sight, until all she could see was whiteness.

Then, ash—falling from the sky all around her like snow. She heard the stomping of hooves, echoing across a rocky chasm. The hooves drew nearer. She turned, but couldn't see them, only the softly falling ash, glinting against a cloudy sky. A shout, a cry for help—she looked behind her to see a man and a boy struggling on a cliff. The man grabbed the boy's arms and forced him back until he was nearly over the edge. It was Bailey, and he was about to die unless Gwen helped him. She ran toward them, her feet slipping on the ashy ground.

Bailey! she cried. *Hold on!*

She beat on the back of the mysterious man with her fists; she grabbed his shoulder and tried to force him to retreat and leave Bailey safe. But, it felt as though she were a ghost, watching her hand pass through a wall. There was no effect. She was not even there.

It's not happening, she thought. This is only a vision. If I can just see the man's face...

Bailey continued to struggle. He was breathing hard, and was no match for the strength of the man who was forcing him, inch by inch, to the cliff's edge.

Gwen ducked as the man bore down on Bailey. She moved so that she could see his face. What she saw made her recoil. The familiar mustache; the sad, tired eyes—it couldn't be true.

"Tremelo!" she cried.

Her eyes opened.

"Ants alive—yes? I'm right here!" Tremelo crouched in front of her, his eyes wide with surprise and concern.

She lay on the ground with her pack open next to her. The Glass still glowed faintly; she closed the flap so no one could see. Phi sat at her side, while Digby, Bailey, Tori, and Hal stood nearby.

"Oh, thank Nature, she's back," wheezed Digby. He held his red wool stocking cap in his hands, wringing it back and forth.

"Are you all right?" asked Phi. "You collapsed."

Gwen sat up with Phi's help. Her hands shook. She couldn't stop the image of Tremelo grappling with Bailey from playing itself over and over in her mind.

"I'm fine," she lied. "Just tired."

She leaned on Phi, who led her out of the workspace. Gwen felt the eyes of Tremelo and RATS bearing down on her.

"She just needs some space," Phi told them, helping her to her feet. She brought Gwen to their sleeping place, which was a cozy nook just around the corner from the tunnel exit. Bailey, Tori, and Hal followed closely.

"Are you okay?" whispered Phi. "Was it a vision?" She eased Gwen down onto her sleeping pallet.

"What do you mean, a 'vision'?" asked Hal, his hearing as acute as ever.

"You're having visions?" said Bailey.

Gwen felt exposed at the mention of them in front of the others. But the sight of Bailey's face—kind, curious—made her last vision all the more harrowing. She couldn't let it happen. She couldn't lose her new friend. The resistance couldn't lose him.

"Yes," she told them shakily. "I'm a Seer. I only found out when Phi and I were in the Peaks."

"And the Glass belongs to her," Phi added.

Gwen nodded. "When I told you at the Fair that the Reckoning was about to begin, it's because I saw it in a vision," Gwen said, still looking at the floor. "My first vision, in the Seer's cave. I knew what was going to happen before it happened."

"Whoa," said Hal. "So, what did you see this time?"

Tremelo is going to try to kill Bailey, she thought, but she didn't dare say it out loud. It couldn't be true—and if it was true, then why would Tremelo do such a thing?

"It wasn't clear," she said. "Some ash. A cloudy sky."

"What does it mean?" Hal asked, pushing up his glasses.

"I think the more constructive question is: Can you tell us where to go? What to do next?" Tori asked. Her eyes were wide, and she seemed genuinely hopeful—which made Gwen feel even worse.

Gwen shook her head and rubbed her temples with her fingertips. She could feel the blood in her head pounding.

"It doesn't work like that," she said. "I can't make myself see something specific."

"Why didn't you tell us?" asked Bailey. He'd been silent, and only now, when he spoke, did she realize he was hurt. "We've been together this whole time...."

"She's only just found out that she's a Seer. She needs time to get used to it," Phi said to Bailey. "And we can't tell the others, either. If the Allies knew, they'd never stop asking her questions."

"I was going to tell you, really I was," Gwen said. "And Tremelo too. But after the Fair..." The memory of Melem the owl screeching at her, how the sound had echoed the same screech she'd heard in her first vision, made Gwen's skin crawl. She had asked Ama, the wise old Seer, if her visions could be changed, and although she had not killed Melem, everything else that had happened to her at the Fair mirrored what she had seen. What did this mean, she wondered, for Bailey? Until she knew for certain, all she could do was try to protect Bailey in any way she could, even if that meant keeping him away from his own mentor. She breathed deep. "I'm sorry I kept it from you."

The others looked at her as though she'd just grown feathers, and they were afraid she'd fly away if frightened. Phi rubbed her back. After a moment, Bailey spoke.

"Well...if you happen to see anything, you'll let us know, right?" he asked.

"Bailey," reprimanded Phi.

"I'm sorry, we just need all the help we can get," Bailey said. "We know Viviana's going to have the power of Dominance on her side, plus whatever those new contraptions her tinkerers are making for her. We've got the bond. But it's not enough! You heard what Merrit said—we need something that can destroy Dominance once and for all! Tremelo can only do so much on his own. There's a whole kingdom out there, full of people who might help us. We need to find them!"

"But what about Viviana's army?" Tori asked. "She's not just fighting with humans; we can expect that much, can't we? She'll be using people's kin!"

"That, and whatever she's making in the Seers' Valley," said Hal.

"That's right," said Tori. "We don't just need an army; we need some kind of weapon."

Gwen imagined a Halcyon machine as large as a rigimotive car, pushed onto a battlefield by Digby and his RATS, and powered by a crank the size of Taleth the white tiger. What such weapon could exist—and what could it do?

"What we need is something that can destroy Dominance, not just heal the bond," said Bailey.

Tori cocked her head at him.

"Say that again?" she asked. She looked at Gwen and made a gesture to her beaded messenger bag.

"We need a weapon that doesn't just heal the bond," Bailey repeated. "Something that can actually cut away at Dominance."

"Ants alive," said Tori. "Gwen—are you thinking what I'm thinking?"

Gwen felt all eyes on her once more. Bailey and Hal raised confused eyebrows, while Tori grinned and nodded at her. Phi simply smiled with support and placed her hand on Gwen's own.

"Well, what do you think?" said Tori.

Gwen nodded. She knew precisely what Tori was thinking. Bailey's words had sounded a bell in Gwen's mind, a bell she knew was ringing in Tori's and Phi's as well.

"It's time to tell him," Gwen said.

Three

"TELL ME WHAT?" BAILEY asked. The girls each looked at him, and then at one another. He immediately felt a strong dislike for the tunnels that had been their home for the past weeks.

"Yeah, tell us what?" asked Hal.

"What's with all the secrets?" Bailey said. Gwen hadn't trusted him enough to tell him she was a Seer. Now what would he learn?

"It's not that we wanted to keep this from you—" said Gwen.

"We just didn't trust you to keep your mouths shut," said Tori.

"—but we wanted to wait until we actually had something of value to share," Gwen finished.

Tori pulled off her beaded bag, which she always wore, messenger-style, around her shoulders. She undid the drawstring, swept away a black snake that slithered from the opening, and took out a familiar leather-bound book with an embossed image of a wild cat—a tiger—on its cover.

"The Loon's book!" Bailey said. "You've had it the whole time?"

Tori smirked.

"When Tremelo and I packed up for the Fair, I didn't think it was right to leave it at the school. Anything could have happened to it!"

"Anything could have happened to it at the Fair, too," said Hal. "You should be glad Viviana didn't find out you had it!"

Tori shot him a narrow-eyed look.

"I was going to give it to you, but then I thought, well, they won't even be able to read it, so I'd better talk to Gwen first—"

"Because I have the Seers' Glass," said Gwen.

"Right," said Tori. "So while you've been playing mini-warriors, we've been looking through it together, trying to find something useful."

Bailey wanted to leap forward and grab the book from Tori's hands. He resisted, but his very skin felt alive with excitement.

"So, have you found something, then?" he asked.

Tori held out the book to him. The leather was soft under his fingers. He traced the embossed creature on the front cover with his finger. He knew now that it was a white tiger—his own Animas. His entire fate was in this book that the Loon had written.

"Give it here," Gwen said.

Reluctantly, Bailey handed the book to her. Gwen set it on her lap and opened it. Bailey sat down next to her and leaned over her shoulder to get a better look. The markings the Loon had made in the book's pages were both familiar and mysterious; like twigs scattered across the ground, the seemingly random symbols made no sense at first glance. But when Gwen guided the Seers' Glass along the open page, it reflected the markings, and, with that reflection, created the form of letters. Bailey mouthed the words together with Gwen.

Sunken deep at kingdom's edge and watched by a wise and dusty army, the True King's symbol of peace waits for its time to sing again. Its song is twofold: to cleave and to bond, to sever and to heal.

"'To sever and to heal,'" repeated Tori. "Just like you said, Bailey."

"But I don't understand," Bailey admitted. "It doesn't say anything about a weapon. How do we know what this 'symbol' is?"

"Does it matter?" said Tori. "It's watched by an army! Maybe that army would fight for Tremelo! Then we have both the symbol *and* the fighters that we need."

"A *dusty* army," said Hal. "Does anyone else think that might mean an army of old people?"

"Or an army we have to fight ourselves, in order to get . . . whatever this thing is!" said Bailey. He glanced down at Gwen for help, but she was busy sliding the Glass along the passage again.

"'At kingdom's edge . . .'" she whispered. "'A wise and dusty army . . .'"

"I think I know what the riddle means!" Phi said. Her tan cheeks were flushed.

"You do?" Bailey asked.

Gwen looked up from the book. Tori and Hal leaned in to hear what Phi would say.

"Sure—just listen," she said. "Gwen, read it again?"

"'Sunken deep at kingdom's edge and watched by a wise and dusty army,'" read Gwen.

"'Sunken deep,' that must mean the ocean," said Phi. "And

'at kingdom's edge,' that means someplace where people don't often go. It must mean the Bay of Braour!"

"Where?" asked Bailey, trying to recall if his mom and dad had ever mentioned such a place to him.

"Don't be silly, we learned about it in History," said Tori. "It's at the far northeastern edge of the Dust Plains. Past the Maze, past the Lowlands—the largest, most unsettled territory in all of Aldermere."

"But why would something of Melore's be all the way out there?" Hal asked. "He wouldn't have spent much time in Braour during his reign. It was completely lawless."

Bailey thought back on everything he knew about the Plains. He and Hal had become far too acquainted with the northern Dust Plains in the weeks before the Reckoning. The thought of a place more remote and more threatening than the Jackal's bunker made his skin crawl. But something else floated to the forefront of his memory, pushing aside the menacing specter of the Jackal: it was the voice of Digby Barnes on the first night they met in the Gudgeons. *No one really knows where Viviana's been since that awful night. Some say she was a slave all those years she was lost; some say she became the leader of an outlaw gang in the Dust Plains.*

"Melore wouldn't have been out there," Bailey said. "But Viviana may have been. She might have left something behind— something of her father's—that now we can use to stop her!"

"I don't know," said Hal. "Maybe we should ask Tremelo?"

"No!"

Bailey and the others looked down at Gwen, who sat clutching the Loon's book to her chest. She blushed.

"Why not?" Bailey asked her.

"I just think..." She paused. One hand traveled to her hair, where she twisted it between her fingers. "He has enough on his mind. I think Phi could be right."

"You mean, you think we should go?" Phi asked. She looked surprised. "Just like that?"

Bailey stared at Gwen. She was undoubtedly a part of their group now, ever since they had all fought together against Miss Sucrette. But Gwen could be such a mystery at times. She caught him looking at her. Something in her eyes fluttered with worry. What, he wondered, had she seen in her vision?

"Yes," she said. "We know what needs to be done for the good of all the Allies. I say we get a good night's sleep and leave before first light."

Bailey looked to Phi, who nodded in assent.

"Another adventure, then!" crowed Tori.

"At least this time, we're all together," Hal said. He smiled at Tori, and to Bailey's surprise, she didn't scowl—but she did cross her arms and look away shyly. Bailey offered Gwen his hand as she stood up and folded the Loon's book into her bag.

"Yes," Gwen agreed. "We're all together."

In the morning, Taleth waited for Bailey outside his sleeping nook. When he emerged with his rucksack to meet the others, she stood and rubbed her forehead against his shoulder.

"You don't mind another journey, do you?" he asked. She didn't, he knew. The walls of the tunnels made her feel too big, and the lack of sunlight made her weary. She wanted to run, to hunt, to see the trees. Bailey scratched behind her large ears. He knew exactly how she felt.

He hurried through the early morning hush of the tunnels toward the girls' sleeping nook, but stopped short when he saw a flicker of candlelight coming from Tremelo's work space. He set his rucksack down against the tunnel wall, out of sight, and peeked around the corner. Tremelo stood over his work, alone. He saw Bailey and waved him into the space.

"Is Gwen all right?" Tremelo asked.

"She's fine," lied Bailey. "Eneas leaving got her upset." Even if he didn't know what was bothering her exactly, it was pretty clear she was not all right. But Tremelo had enough on his mind.

Tremelo tapped his knuckles on his worktable. "I'm afraid I haven't been as attentive to the needs of you young ones as I should be," he said. "You shouldn't have to be worried about Eneas, or anything for that matter. I should have tried to shield you from all that."

"No," said Bailey. "We want to help!" He wondered if Gwen was right to say that Tremelo shouldn't know about their plans to journey to the Dust Plains.

Tremelo shook his head.

"I can't let you do that."

Bailey swallowed his next words. He'd wanted to blurt out the entire plan—the trek to the Plains, the riddle of the book, Gwen's visions, everything.

"I'm sending Digby and the RATS out into the Lowlands and the villages between the Peaks and the Gray to drum up support," Tremelo said. "They leave any moment now. And until I can make more of these"—he swept his hand over a pile of the amulets he'd made, about a dozen in all—"then that will have to do. In the meantime, the tunnels are the safest place to be until we can amass more fighters."

"What if..." Bailey began. "What if there was a different army—one we haven't thought of yet. If you knew where they might be, wouldn't you want to find them?"

Tremelo raised one black eyebrow and folded his arms.

"Did you speak with Eneas?" he asked.

Confused, Bailey shook his head.

"Eneas? Why?"

"What did he say to you?" Tremelo asked. He searched Bailey's face, but Bailey wasn't sure what he was looking for. He had spoken to Eneas before the warrior had left the camp, but what of that could cause Tremelo such concern?

"Whatever he told you, don't take it to heart," Tremelo said. "The Velyn have many strange superstitions in their culture. Stories. Stories won't save us. This will." He pointed to the amulets again and breathed a heavy sigh. "These are dangerous times," he continued. "We must keep working where we are sure we can gain ground. Not go off chasing dreams."

Bailey wanted to ask what dreams had caused such a divide between Tremelo and Eneas, but he didn't have the chance. Just then, Digby Barnes hastened into the room. His makeshift metal armor clanged and squeaked as he clapped Bailey on the back and shook Tremelo's hand.

"Well, we're off," he said. "I've got some o' the troops heading down into the Lowlands to rally with Roger, and the rest of us is going up Stillfall way. Anyone we meet, we'll send back here. You sure you don't want more of us to stay with you? Now that Eneas is gone . . ."

"The Velyn here are trustworthy," Tremelo said firmly. "I have no doubt on that score, no matter what the others say. I will be fine here."

"That may be true, sir," said Digby. He patted down his red wool cap and lowered an absurd helmet made of flattened soup cans onto his head. "But you send word to Roger if that changes." He shook Tremelo's hand again.

"Bailey, I trust you'll take care of our regal highness while I'm gone." Digby shook Bailey's hand as well, and gave Taleth a swift pet on the top of her head.

"I'll try," Bailey said. The lie made his stomach churn.

"I'll see you off," said Tremelo. He followed the clattering Digby out of the workspace and into the tunnels.

"When I was just a ferret's size," Digby sang as he exited, "my mum said to me, 'Son! Don't pull the tail of a RAT in his hole, or you'll find the fight's been won!'"

Bailey watched them go, his guilt and confusion eating away at his previous excitement about the new adventure he and his friends had concocted. What was it that had wedged such a rift between Eneas and Tremelo? And why, once again, did Tremelo not want his help? He looked down at the worktable, where the metal glint of the amulets caught his eye. His heart stirred. Tremelo would worry about them all, once he realized they were gone. But if he knew that they had some small protection, perhaps next time he wouldn't accuse Bailey of never thinking before taking action.

Bailey grabbed three of the amulets and stuffed them into his coat pocket. Just like Tremelo, he would do what he needed to keep his friends safe. Surely Tremelo would understand.

Once he was certain that Digby and Tremelo were out of sight, he grabbed his rucksack and hurried to meet the others.

Four

TREMELO MIGHT HAVE LAUGHED, once, at the sight of the RATS in their traveling gear. All done up in sheets of metal tied with rope, and sporting weapons like slatted spoons and hand-knotted nets in addition to their bows and arrows and knives, Digby's crew made for a motley sight. But Tremelo couldn't quite remember the last time he'd laughed at anything—not since he had brought his followers to these dark, dusty tunnels. Certainly not since Eneas Fourclaw, his only hope for gaining the trust and loyalty of the Velyn, had disappeared without even a fare-you-well.

"Be back before you know it!" Digby lifted his hand to his forehead in a jaunty salute. Then, with the rest of the RATS, he began a cautious climb down the steep hill toward the Lowlands.

Tremelo fought the urge to call out *"Be careful!"*—as if they needed reminding. He ached for a myrgwood pipe. His faith that

Digby would find anyone in the RATS network willing to risk their lives for him was wearing away. He tried to hold on to hope he'd been carrying inside him since the evening of the Reckoning; huddled in the Gray City RATS Nest, hearing his newfound followers' cheers for him, for their king, had made him believe that Viviana's defeat would be swift and soon. But now, with Eneas gone and the Velyn unmoored, his hope was dwindling as quickly as their chances.

Fennel the fox waited for him on the path. She sat licking her black paws, still red with the blood of a bird she'd eaten for breakfast. Tremelo's own stomach grumbled.

As he neared the tunnel entrance he heard a rustling noise, then a whisper. He hurried around the next tree and saw three Velyn women with packs on their backs. They froze when they noticed him.

"What's going on?" he asked. "Has something happened?"

The women looked at one another. Finally, the one closest to him, a young fighter with red hair bound up on her head, spoke.

"We're not staying," she said. "Some of the others are, but it's only a matter of time. We'd rather take our chances in the woods."

"You can't leave," Tremelo said. "Please—Eneas will be back. Don't you want to stand up to Viviana?"

The red-haired woman jutted out her chin.

"Viviana isn't after us the way the Jackal was. She wants you. We were safer before we joined you."

She nodded to her companions, and together they began to climb up the rocks that led farther up into the Peaks.

"Wait!" Tremelo cried. "Don't you understand? Dominance is

a threat to all of us! You won't be able to hide if we can't defeat it. We have to stay together!"

The women didn't stop climbing. Soon enough they disappeared over the rocks and into the trees. A murder of crows lit up from the branches of those trees, circled once overhead, and followed the women.

"Ants, ants, *ants*," Tremelo cursed. He ducked into the tunnel, listening for the other Velyn. Dogs barked; an owl hooted. The others in the tunnel were awake and restless. He passed a huddled group of men and women on whom he could direct his wrath. "What good is *strategy* and *caution*," he demanded, his arms flailing as he spoke, "when all one has to do is skip into the woods and find a make-believe army?!"

The group had gone quiet, and looked up at him now.

"Why even bother trying to save the kingdom?" he said, then wheeled off toward his work space to think.

He was acting rashly. He knew that, just as well as he knew all the reasons that the kingdom was worth saving, worth fighting for. But he was angry, and felt betrayed. He couldn't be sure if Eneas would return. What kind of king would he be, if he couldn't convince his allies and followers that his plan was the way to victory?

But Eneas's disappearance made Tremelo second-guess himself. Eneas had tried convincing Tremelo to move south, beyond the Peaks. But there was nothing beyond the Peaks, Tremelo knew this. Only wilderness, and the kind of tall tales that are exciting to tell around a fire but useless in the face of real war. The Queen of the Underlands, indeed. Tremelo sat down and placed his head in his hands.

"What am I going to do?" he asked Fennel. She sat at his feet and gazed up at him. Her black eyes were bottomless—she couldn't help him, either. She sniffed the air and then jumped up onto the table.

"What is it?" he groaned. He felt a prickling of worry in the way her fur ruffed at the neck. She began to whine.

He looked at where her nose was pointed on the worktable: the pile of amulets he'd made had been disturbed. Quickly, he counted. Three were missing.

"Did I give them to Digby?" he asked aloud. Fennel cocked her head. He knew he hadn't. All of the amulets had been here when he'd left Bailey in the room that morning.

"No . . ." he said, launching himself off of his stool and running for the boys' sleeping nook. "Bailey!" he cried. But all that greeted him in the nook was a discarded sleeping roll, an extinguished torch leaning against the wall, and a note.

We've gone to find you an army, it said.

Tremelo stuffed the note into the breast pocket of his worn striped vest and ran to the girls' quarters, knowing what he'd find. Sure enough, Gwen, Tori, and Phi had left the same sparse disarray behind: a few scraps of clothing, a few eating utensils borrowed from Digby's supplies, and another doused torch.

"Fools," Tremelo spat. He looked down at Fennel. "Let's go; we may still be able to track them!" He ran outside with Fennel at his heels. The tops of the trees were now orange with the rising sun.

Fennel dashed into the brush; her black nose and her whiskers quivered. Tremelo held his hand over his heart, which hammered like an engine in his chest. Once again, Bailey had betrayed his good judgment and run off. How many times would the boy need saving before it was too late? He tried to quiet his mind and find Fennel. She was running fast; her heart beat as audibly as his. She smelled the students, but more than them, she smelled the strong scent of Taleth. They were headed down the mountain, in the opposite direction of Digby and his RATS. They were going east. Why? He felt himself pulled forward by Fennel's energy. She had the scent—he followed it down the hill, weaving between the pines. Bailey always acted on instinct, and now Tremelo's own instinct told him to keep the boy safe at all costs. He stumbled over a root but righted himself and surged forward. Fennel ran ahead, just out of sight.

He closed his eyes, feeling his consciousness flicker in and out as he tapped into the bond. A switch occurred, and Tremelo felt himself one with Fennel. He didn't hear or see the person behind him, but smelled them as Fennel did. When she stopped short on the path with a frightened yip, Tremelo was blinded by his own adrenaline and panic. And then all was darkness—a bag was pulled over his head and he was dragged away from the path, away from Fennel, into the heavy brush of the woods. He kicked against the dirt and the leaves, but the person holding him was strong. And he was dragged away as he heard Fennel whine. Searching his mind for her, he could find nothing. She was gone. A chilly breeze rustled through the pine trees, unfriendly and cold.

Five

"I HATE TO BE the one to say it," said Tori as the kids trudged along a back road in the Lowlands. "But we can't exactly buy rigi tickets for five schoolkids and their pet white tiger. I have a sneaky feeling the Dominae might be, I don't know, looking for that *exact* thing."

They were headed to a station that serviced a trade rigi bound for the southern Dust Plains. The Bay of Braour was located at the far northeast coast of Aldermere, and though the southern Plains were reportedly more barren—and more dangerous—than the north, after some discussion Bailey and his friends knew they had no choice but to cross them.

"At least the southbound rigis are mostly grains and goods," said Bailey. "No passengers. We just have to sneak on."

"It'd be more dangerous to take the rigi the other direction through the Gray," Hal added. "They'd be searching every car for us!"

It was common knowledge that the rigimotive, which had been designed to run in a great circle through the kingdom, was more like a crescent moon. Its western route ended in the northern Dust Plains just outside the Maze, and the unfinished eastern route, which ran closest to the Lowlands, ended in the midst of the much wilder, much dustier southeastern Plains. In between, the Plains had to be crossed by wagon, motorbuggy, or foot. Bailey's mom and dad had sent grain out that way to be traded with the villages in the eastern Lowlands and the Plains border. Bailey knew that they could ride the rigi there—they just had to avoid getting caught on board.

"I have an idea of how to get on without being seen," said Bailey. "It's going to take a little practice, though."

They had covertly hidden some supplies from the tunnels in their rucksacks and coats: some dried fruit from Digby Barnes's stores, a spare dynamo lamp, and of course, Bailey's tiger claw and three of Tremelo's new amulets. After leaving the tunnels, they'd skirted the edge of the forest, keeping their ears sharp for any Dominae who might be searching the woods. Now, as they passed so close to the Walkers' wheat fields, Bailey felt heartsick. Somewhere close by, his mom and dad might be hearing the rumors of a boy and white tiger wanted by the Dominae. Did they know that those rumors were about the boy they'd raised as their own? Were they worried about him?

They trudged along back roads, heading northeast from the forest to the rigi tracks. To board at an actual stop would be far too dangerous—instead, Bailey led them a few miles away from the nearest town to a switch-track point, where the cargo rigis would need to slow their speed in order to pass through safely. Here, they paused to rest and plan behind a sweeping ridge of bushes that grew along the tracks.

"Okay," said Bailey, steeling his nerves. "Here's my idea."

He watched his friends' faces grow slack with disbelief and nervous fear as he described how they'd get onto the rigi. He knew it was dangerous—but as Tori had said, they couldn't very well go to a station and buy tickets.

"We could get hurt—or killed," said Gwen.

"Do *you* have another idea?" asked Tori with a bite in her voice. Gwen didn't respond.

"We can do it," said Phi. "It's just like Scavage."

"Right!" said Bailey, eager to grasp onto someone's hope. "Exactly."

"Some of us didn't make the team, remember?" said Hal.

"Don't worry," said Tori. "We can go together."

"And we'll practice," said Bailey. "Just to make sure."

An hour later, after they'd taken turns running and jumping over a pile of abandoned shipping pallets by the switch track, Bailey sensed an anxious energy from Taleth. She wasn't alone, either— Tori's snakes slithered up her leg from the grass where they'd been sunning and into the beaded pouch she wore across her back.

"I think the rigi's coming," Tori said. "We'd better get ready."

"We need to space ourselves out, hide in the bushes as it comes," Hal said, indicating their position along the tracks. "Bailey, you'll need to jump on first, in order for Taleth to follow. Then we'll all hop on." They were all nervous about what they were preparing to do, but a kind of excited, electrified energy ran through them, making them bold. They moved silently into the bushes, several yards apart.

Soon enough, they could hear the chug of a cargo rigi approaching. Bailey breathed deeply as the dirigible appeared on the horizon, and then the chugging engine below it. Cargo rigis weren't as tall as passenger rigis, with only one story of boxcars and slabs for transporting heavy goods. The engine slowed as it neared the switch track ahead, and Bailey took off running in the direction of a boxcar with an open door.

As he ran, he was painfully aware of how tired his legs were. They felt as though they might buckle underneath him, and he kept his eyes trained on the ledge of the boxcar door as he raced forward. He grabbed the ledge, and jumped, holding on to the side of the door for his life. His right leg swung over, and he pushed himself up, tumbling through the opening and breathing heavily. He didn't have time to grasp his bearings—the others followed close behind. Looking out, he could see them running too, and his heart beat wildly. The jump had been even harder than he'd thought. His chest burned from where he'd dragged himself up onto the ledge, and his arms ached.

Taleth was next: she leapt for the ledge and sank her claws into the floor. Her back paws gave way and flailed. But with a huff of breath, she threw her right paw forward, grabbing at the floorboards of the car. Bailey wanted to help, but didn't know how—he couldn't take her paws or she'd rip him to shreds, and she was far too heavy for him to pull. He felt her struggling, felt the frenzied motion of her tail lashing in the wind. She scrambled, snorting with the effort as she tried to pull her giant body into the car. Her massive claws dug into the floor of the car, one in front of the other. She strained her muscles and heaved herself on board, making Bailey scramble backward to leave room for her to land.

Gwen, Tori, Hal, and Phi were now running alongside the train. Taleth jumped aside as Bailey reached his hand out the door to help Gwen. Up she came, and then Tori, who cursed loudly as soon as she was safely on board. Hal needed both Bailey and Gwen to grab his arms and pull him on after he couldn't swing his leg up, and he groaned with pain from his shoulder. Then it was just Phi. Carin flew overhead as the rigi began to pick up speed. Phi ran faster, and grabbed a handle on the side of the boxcar as the rigi sped forward. It began to drag her along, and she screamed.

"Phi!" Bailey yelled. He reached his hand out as far as it could go.

"Hold on to him!" Tori shouted, and she grabbed Bailey's waist and motioned for Gwen to grab on to her. With their help, Bailey extended his arm and upper body out of the boxcar door. The wind began to whip by, and he could hear the awful churning of the wheels below them. Phi was grasping the handle with both hands, her legs dangling below.

"Swing yourself forward!" Bailey shouted.

Slowly and fearfully, Phi released her right hand from the handle and grabbed the edge of the doorframe. Bailey grasped at her jacket.

"Now just put your hand on my shoulder," he said. She did, and Bailey backed up. As Phi let go of the handle with her other hand, she fell slightly, causing Bailey to stumble. She screamed, but they kept ahold of each other. Tori and Gwen pulled behind him, and they all landed in a tumbled pile on the boxcar floor.

"Ants alive," said Tori as she leaned against Hal. Bailey saw him stiffen up for a split second before he put his arm around her shoulder.

"You okay?" Hal asked.

"Oh, sure," she said. "I just jumped onto a moving rigi and saw my life flash before my eyes. But, yeah, I'm okay."

"Let's never do that again!" Gwen exclaimed, sitting up.

Phi was still holding Bailey tightly, as though she was afraid to let go. He squeezed her so hard he was sure she'd feel his pounding heart through his chest.

"It's okay; we're okay," he said into her curly hair.

"Thank you," she whispered, loosening her grip.

Tori and Gwen crawled over and peeled Phi away from Bailey, collapsing onto her in a giant pile of hugs. The exhaustion hit Bailey, and all of a sudden, he just wanted to close his eyes and sleep. The girls separated. Tori joined Hal where he sat holding his shoulder against a stack of crates. Phi and Gwen sat down, arm in arm, next to Bailey.

"I'll keep watch," said Phi. "You two can sleep."

Bailey didn't need to be told twice. As the girls used a loose tarp as a blanket, Bailey curled up into a ball and closed his eyes tightly, willing sleep to come quickly. Taleth, purring with relief, eased down next to him. The rougher fur on the back of her neck was bristly against his cheek. He heard the comforting screech of Carin, Phi's kin, circling the boxcars. Lulled by the steady shaking of the rigi, he fell into a deep, dreamless sleep for the first time in many weeks.

When he woke, Phi was sitting up, looking out at the sky. It had dimmed to a purplish sunset blue.

"Did you get a chance to rest?" he asked her. Everyone else was still sleeping.

Phi shook her head. "I couldn't sleep. And anyway, Gwen took the entire blanket," she said with a smile. "I should've gotten used to it after all the camping we did in the Peaks, but she's a hog."

Bailey peered over to Phi's other side, where Gwen had wrapped herself tightly in the crunchy tarp. She frowned in her sleep.

"She okay?" Bailey asked. Something had been troubling her.

Phi nodded thoughtfully. "She's having a hard time, but she'll be okay, I think."

"And you? Are you going to be okay?"

Phi shrugged and looked away. "Back there, I was scared you might let go...."

Bailey sat up. "I would've never let go!"

"I know that, Bailey," she said, meeting his eye. "Of course I know that. I just meant, what if you couldn't help it? I wished more than anything that I could fly at that moment. That I could save myself if I needed to...."

Bailey remembered the contraption Phi had made with Tremelo's help. How she'd built that intricate machine with its tarp wings, and how she'd crashed it during the thunderstorm. Before he could say anything more, she stood up. Gwen woke from Phi's sudden movement. Tori and Hal stirred.

"We've got to hop off soon," Phi called out. "We're coming up on the final stop, and we don't want to be seen near the station."

Taleth rose and stretched, lashing her tail. Bailey sat up too, and looked out the open door of the car. The southern Plains were as flat as a long harvest table, and just as brown. Unlike the dry, grassy hills of the Plains surrounding the Jackal's compound, these eastern Plains were pure desert.

"Do we really need to worry about the station?" he asked. "Who would be out this far?"

"Better safe than sorry," Phi said. " I don't know how it works down here, but up north, there are usually bands of traders waiting at the last stop to divide up the shipments—or just steal them."

They waited until the train began to slow. One by one they sprang from the open car doors. The kids each landed with a rolling thump in the sand, followed by Taleth, who sprang gracefully and landed on all fours. The train chugged on, leaving them sprawled on the ground and gasping from the adrenaline.

They decided to circumvent the station and then follow the miles of abandoned rigi tracks that lay unused beyond the final stop. It would be dangerous—many traders and thieves made their homes out there—but traveling by night meant less chance of being seen. After bypassing the station, which was a single one-room building with a lone swinging gas lamp on a hook, they walked along the tracks for what seemed like many miles. The sky darkened, and Bailey could see more stars overhead than he'd ever seen in his life. He was glad to still be wearing his coat, too—the temperature dropped sharply after the last bit of sun disappeared.

The desert was silent and cold, and Bailey felt a little like he and his friends had been placed in another world, as though the rigi had carried him out of his own plane of existence and set him down in a place of possibility, where perhaps the Reckoning hadn't happened at all, and the kingdom around them was at peace. Or maybe the night air was only playing tricks with his tired mind.

After many hours of trudging in silence, a line of pale light streaked the sky ahead.

"The sun must be rising," said Hal. "It doesn't really seem like we've walked all night, does it?"

"Time flies," murmured Tori.

Phi stopped in her tracks and placed a hand on Bailey's arm.

"That's not the sunrise," she said. Bailey heard a wavering note of fear in her voice. He followed her gaze out toward the horizon. The band of pale-gray light, like a cloudy dawn, grew larger. It was as though the night sky above them was a dark-blue curtain in the process of being slowly raised. Then he heard the wind.

"It's a sandstorm!" said Phi. "Run!"

Mesmerized, Bailey stood in place. He'd never seen anything like this before: the strip of gray cutting across the bottom of the sky grew larger and seemed to glow with a greenish, eerie light. It would bury them alive, leaving no trace of them on the ground's surface.

"Bailey, come on!" Phi pulled at his arm. The others were running full tilt away from the approaching storm. Bailey ran with them, holding Phi's hand.

Gwen and Taleth were in front. Suddenly, they stopped short, and Bailey felt the hair on the back of his neck prickle—Taleth was panicked.

"Stop!" shouted Gwen, holding out her hands to catch Tori as she sped up to her. When Bailey reached them, he understood why: they were standing on the edge of a deep ravine, a steep drop that plummeted down, down into a canyon below. The kids turned to watch the sandstorm growing larger and closer—only as far away from them now as the length of a Scavage pitch. Bailey could feel the wind picking up, and whirling twisters of sand were visible only a few feet away.

"What do we do?" Bailey asked.

Tori cried out suddenly—one of her slim, black snakes had fallen to the ground and was winding its way to the cliff's edge. Tori crouched, trying to catch it, but it slipped over the edge.

"Look!" she said, pointing. The snake wound its way along a narrow path of rocks, and then disappeared into the wall of the cliff.

"Come on," said Tori. "There's something down here." She eased herself over the edge, wincing as she stretched out her toes to feel for the foothold. The she dropped onto the rocks jutting out from the cliff.

"Yes—it's a cave!" she called up.

"Go, go!" shouted Phi. The storm was on them—sand whipping around, stinging their faces and arms. The kids followed Tori, scrambling over the side of the cliff, holding fast to the rocks, into the safety of the cave. Carin overshot the cave entrance and met resistance in the wind as she turned around and tried to come back, flapping her wings hard as her feathers streamed. Eventually, she lowered and dove into the cave, her talons clutching into the leather on Phi's arm. Only Taleth remained, her massive paws at the edge. She was scared. Bailey could feel it. He closed his eyes and tried to think calm thoughts as she turned around and lowered her hind legs off the cliff, pawing at the air as her front legs hung on. Everyone moved back.

"Come on, Taleth," Bailey whispered. She slipped lower and

lower, but it was too dangerous to grab for her, and he had to trust. Then in one graceful move, she threw her weight into the cave, landing with a thud. Bailey collapsed on top of her.

Once they were inside, the wave of sand came pouring past the opening and across the howling ravine. Phi sat next to Bailey and Taleth, and Bailey's hand found Phi's again.

"You saved me back there," he told her. "Thank you."

"We're even now," she said. He thought how they'd never really be even; she'd always saved him, even before she really knew him, back when the only saving he needed was from Taylor Quindley's barbed taunts.

She smiled and squeezed his hand. Bailey wanted to hug her, or maybe even kiss her, but he didn't dare move. He just watched the way she shrugged her curly hair off of her thin shoulders, and he felt himself blushing.

He heard commotion farther in the cavern, and saw a spark of light.

"It looks like the others have gotten a fire going," he said. "Let's go warm up."

Phi nodded and let go of his hand. He tried to hide his disappointment as they walked to join their friends and kin, ignoring the howling of the wind and the raw pelting of the sand outside. It felt as though they were sitting in the middle of a raging war, with Nature doing battle against itself. Bailey shuddered. At least for now, he and his friends were safe. But when the storm cleared, another war waited.

Six

THE FOX DASHED THROUGH the woods, panicked. Leaves and twigs swatted her nose and eyes, the wind whistled in her ears, created by her own furious running. Her kin was just ahead, always just out of reach—she couldn't catch up. She couldn't stop him.

He was afraid. Tremelo was afraid. The fur on her nape stiffened. She could feel his dismay as he struggled with the ropes binding his hands. She sensed the wetness of his own breath building behind the cloth gag fitted around his mouth. *I'm coming; I'm coming*: the refrain beat along with her quickly pounding heart.

Go back.

But she ran harder, the pain intensifying in her tender paw.

Go back, Fennel.

She kept running, ignoring him and his insistent thoughts.

Go back. Lead them to me. Help them find me.

With a dismayed bark of alarm, Fennel stopped running. She

panted for fresh air in her burning lungs. Her ribs and her paws ached. She shook herself violently. He was afraid, but he wanted her to leave him.

She took a deep, cold breath and let out a high-pitched howl. In the deep woods, she heard it echoed back to her by other foxes who had sensed Tremelo passing through the woods, and sensed his fear along with hers. The echoes followed her, almost taunting her, as she raced in the direction from which she'd come.

When she reached the tunnels again to search for help, she found no one.

Seven

BAILEY WOKE TO WHAT he believed to be morning—but no light shone from the entrance to the cave to prove him right. He and his friends had all been huddled together for warmth, and when he stood up he shivered. The entrance through which they'd come the night before was dark, entirely blocked off by a wall of sand and rocks. Taleth rose, stretched, and padded after him to investigate.

Bailey pushed aside some of the rocks, only to have more tumble after them into the cavern entrance. He felt a heavy shifting as some rocks fell on the other side of the pile. A small pinprick of light broke through. He kept trying until he could pull his shoulders to the outside.

The ledge outside the entrance was entirely destroyed—the only few feet that remained were obstructed by heavy rocks that had fallen from the cliff's edge in the night, toppled by the power-ful sandstorm. And below was a drop that would easily kill them. He craned his neck to look up to the cliff top—too far and too steep to climb. They couldn't get out the way they'd come.

He eased back into the cavern to see the others sitting up, rub-bing the sleep out of their eyes.

"We're trapped." As he said it he realized how dire the situ-ation actually was—they could starve in here if they didn't find another way out. The others stared at him as though he'd just said something in an entirely new language.

"What do you mean?" asked Hal, rushing to the opening. He pushed his glasses onto his nose and leaned his head out.

"Careful!" said Bailey. "The ledge is gone."

Hal stepped back, his face slack and pale. "What are we going to do?"

"We . . . we could try to climb up the rock face," said Bailey. He leaned out of the opening again to take a look at the vertical rock face above them. "Unless we can find a rope . . ."

"The thing about ropes is that you need something to tie them *to*," Tori said from behind them.

"There might be something," Bailey said, scanning the sharp edge of the cliff.

"Doubtful," said Hal, blinking behind his glasses. "With the constant sandstorms, erosion is inevitable, and—"

"We're *stuck* is what you guys are saying," said Gwen, squeez-ing through to look down the cliff. She shook her head in disbelief.

"Carin could fly out, search for something we could use," Phi offered from behind them. The falcon dug her talons firmly into the leather patch on Phi's shoulder.

"Which would be what, exactly? There's nothing out there that's not buried in sand at this point. And we left that tarp in the rigi," Tori said with a weary sigh. "We weren't thinking."

"We could call for help!" Hal said, clambering back over the pile of rocks in front of the entrance.

"You'll let every lowlife in the area know we're here if you do that," said Tori.

"We've got to try!" said Hal. "I know you don't want to starve in a cave, even if it *does* mean you're right about something."

Tori shot him an irritated look. "There's got to be something we're not thinking of," she said. Her snakes emerged from her beaded bag and slithered down to the floor of the cave. They stayed close to the wall, anxiously slithering in wide S curves.

"Oh, *ants*," breathed Gwen, taking Bailey by surprise—he'd never heard her curse before. "This can't be right," she said, stumbling to the interior wall of the cavern. She sank down into a crouch. "It can't end *here*."

"What do you mean, *end*?" Phi asked, stomping over and squatting down next to her. "We're not going to die here. We just haven't found the solution yet!"

Bailey looked around at each of his friends, taking in the apprehension, fear, and frustration he saw on their faces. Gwen was right—it couldn't end here.

"I'll climb out," he said. "If I can get to the top, maybe I can find something to help lift the rest of you out—a branch or some rope. I'll be careful."

"Ants, Bailey, don't be stupid," said Hal. "You don't always have to be the hero."

"What's that supposed to mean?" Bailey felt Taleth's breath on the back of his neck. She nudged his shoulder with her forehead, concerned. "What, you're taking his side?" he asked Taleth.

"It's not about sides, Bailey. It's a crazy idea," Tori said, her arms crossed.

"Tigers are great climbers," Bailey said forcefully. "It'll come naturally to me."

He pushed past Hal and Tori, and eased himself through the opening. Everyone protested at once, but he tuned them out. He refused to look down as he grabbed ahold of a nick in the rock face and pressed himself frontward against the cliff. With his right foot, he felt around for the surface of one of the fallen rocks. As soon as the ball of his foot connected, he carefully let his weight slide away from the cave entrance, where two heads—Hal's and Taleth's—poked out, watching.

At first, the rock seemed stable. He felt a trill of hope in his chest—he'd show them he would make it! But as soon as he moved his left hand away from the edge of the opening, he felt a sickening shift beneath him. There was nothing for his left hand to grab on to, and as the boulder wobbled, he cried out. The rock teetered, and Bailey slipped, hanging on with one hand. Suddenly, there was nothing under his feet, and he jolted downward. Something caught him by his shirt collar, and he watched as the boulder tumbled down, down the side of the cliff until he could barely see it. His heart was racing and he saw spots, adrenaline causing his vision to cloud.

He looked up—Taleth had him, his collar in her teeth. All he saw were her whiskers and the side of her face as he glanced over his shoulder. Looking slightly down, he saw her claws dug into the rubble, scrambling to lift him back through the opening. She drew him back into the safety of the cave, where she dropped him, gasping, onto the floor.

"If I wasn't so happy you survived, I'd kill you!" shrieked Tori, suddenly standing over him. They'd all been shouting, gathered by the opening. He'd hardly registered their voices over the blood pumping through his ears.

"Are you all right?" asked Gwen, her face white as paper.

Phi stood with her hand over her mouth, not saying a word—but Carin flew in circles in the small, enclosed space.

Hal gripped Bailey's shoulders so tight it was like a vise closing in around him. "He's fine. You're fine, right?" said Hal, kneeling next to him. He seemed out of breath. "Ants. *Ants.* You're okay."

"Right. Right, I'm okay," Bailey said, his heart still beating out of control. He looked back up at Hal. "Are you going to tell me 'I told you so'?"

Hal shook his head. "I'll just say it was not your brightest idea. It's up there with jumping off the clock tower."

Bailey managed a smile, and everyone stayed silent as the sting of panic eased away. Bailey's heart finally returned to something close to its normal rhythm.

"No one's going near that ledge again," said Phi. "But there's another way. There has to be."

"So what is it, then?" said Tori. "We can't get out the way we came, and if we call for help, we'll only get picked up by someone who—chances are—would rather kill us than help us. Please, Phi, tell us what the brilliant solution is!"

"You don't have to be like that," Phi said. Bailey knew that she was used to Tori's prickly nature, but this was more than every-day bickering between friends. Their lives depended on them not giving up.

"Like what, exactly?" said Tori. She was on her feet now, pacing frantically. "A tiny bit upset that maybe we might die in a cave? Bailey almost just fell off a *cliff*, but I don't have to be upset! No, no, a solution will materialize, if we all stand here wringing our hands about it long enough!" She picked up one of the rocks that had tumbled in from the entrance. With a yell, she threw it, hard, against the back wall of the cave. Dust crumbled down from where it struck, leaving a gray scar in red rock.

"Okay, stop it," said Hal. "This isn't helping anything!"

Tori picked up another rock. The rest of them instinctively drew back. "CHEER UP, TORI!" she yelled. "Why are you always so moody? Why can't you just be happy?!"

She paused, gave an exaggerated smile, then hurled the rock at the same spot. It bounced off, and more dust crumbled from overhead.

"Tori, I didn't mean it that way—" Phi began. But Carin let out a *kak*ing sound that drowned out her voice. Taleth, too, seemed jittery: she left Bailey's side and began pacing, just out of Tori's throwing path.

Bailey had never seen Tori so angry. Sarcastic, standoffish, and irritated, yes, but never angry. But the same could be said for Phi.

"Hey!" she called as she stalked over to where Tori stood. "I've never said anything like that to you! I've never even *thought* it." Phi picked up her own rock and launched it at the same spot on the wall. This one caused a spray of powdery dust to explode from the impact point. Taleth backed away, whiskers shuddering.

"That's the spirit!" Tori said fiercely. Bailey couldn't tell if she was angry or happy or both.

Taleth paced and stared at the spot where Tori's rock ricocheted off the wall of the cave. Her whiskers were twitching up and down, up and down. She was interested in something. Bailey remembered how, when the Jackal had kidnapped her, she had rubbed against the bars of her cage—but this felt different. She moved with purpose now, not agitation. Gwen stood next to him and clutched his shoulder, noticing, too, how Taleth moved.

"You're not the only one, you know," Phi grumbled to Tori. She picked up two rocks and handed one over to her. "Adults telling me to speak up, to not be so shy..." The two girls lifted their rocks in unison.

"Tori, stop!" Both Bailey and Gwen cried out at the same time. Bailey walked forward and touched the nick Phi had made with his finger.

"It's not solid!" he said, wiping his fingers together. A pale dust fell from his hand.

"It's some kind of mineral buildup," said Hal, stepping forward to take a better look. "That means there might be space behind here. There's no moisture on this side, so it stands to reason that on the other side—"

He was cut off by a massive crash. Phi hadn't waited a moment to hurl the rock in her hand at the wall with all her strength. Hal, Bailey, and Gwen backed away as dust and rock particles launched out at them.

"Hey!" said Hal.

"Get out of the way!" Tori yelled. Her anger had shifted, and Bailey could see a resurfacing of the old Tori—mischievous, brazen—taking its place. Now she was having fun. She took the fist-sized rock in her own hand and wound up.

"Look out!" Bailey said, pulling the others away. He thought Tori would've been a great Scavage player as she sent the rock zinging against the wall. More dust crumbled away, and there appeared a spot of darkness—a hole.

"Come on!" said Phi. Together, they all rushed at the wall, using stones to chip away at it until it finally crumbled, revealing a dark passageway. They could smell moisture, and felt cool air emanating from the opening. Far ahead, down the dark hallway of solid rock, was a tiny glow of daylight.

"What did I tell you?" said Tori, charging forward with her dynamo lamp at the ready.

"That was just luck," said Hal, but Phi shot him a look.

Tori's snakes slithered ahead over the rocks, and Bailey and the rest followed.

Passing through the narrow opening in the rock almost made Bailey homesick for the Allies' tunnels. This was small and cramped, and they needed the dynamo lamp to see more than a foot in front of their faces. They shuffled in single file, with Bailey and Taleth in the rear. Taleth followed behind him, barely able to squeeze through. Phi walked just in front of him.

"I didn't know you felt that way," he told her as they walked. "What you said, back there in the cave . . ."

She shrugged. He wished he could make out her face. "Doesn't everyone feel that way? Like they're always being told what to do and how to act?"

He wanted to ask her what she meant, but the dim, bluish

light ahead grew larger; the tunnel opened up into another cavern, where a crack in the rocks let through a slant of sunlight.

On the floor was an unoccupied bedroll and a small, organized pile of foodstuff—a box of pancake powder, a packet of dried cactus, and a few sundry pieces of fruit.

"Someone lives here," Bailey whispered.

"They don't just live here—look," said Phi. She pointed to the other side of the cavern, where several grubby bags were piled, full of shiny new pots and pans, jewelry, and other goods. "It's a smuggler stop!"

They fell upon the food goods, popping the fruit into their rucksacks. Bailey eagerly pocketed the bag of dried cactus.

"Is there any water?" asked Hal, looking around. Bailey didn't see any—no canteens, no buckets. Nothing. They were days, at least, from the Bay of Braour. No one knew how much shelter they would have from the sun. Dried pancake powder was one thing, but water was quite another. He exchanged a glance with Phi, who seemed to be thinking the same thing. There was nothing to do but keep going.

"This way," said Tori, following her snakes as the tunnel continued.

The tunnel, a little wider on this end, slanted upward, and Bailey felt the air becoming warmer as they moved toward the surface of the cliffs once more. Finally, they reached a curve in the stone wall, illuminated by morning sunshine. The entrance was only blocked by a pile of sand, easily swept away. Bailey followed Tori out onto the hot, flat terrain, careful not to step too close to the ravine's edge.

"Well, hello!" came a voice. "Got some mice scuttling in the old homestead!"

Bailey turned to his right, and his stomach fell as he saw two figures leaning on a boulder just a few yards from the entrance. The first man was tall and ruddy, with patchy black stubble on his cheeks and neck. The other was a chinless, somewhat fat, little man wearing a large hat that shielded his small, round eyes.

"And what would you be doing—" The tall man stopped short as Taleth emerged from the tunnel.

"Creaking frogs," muttered the short man, in his own creaking voice. "The stories from the Fair . . . they're true. . . ."

"You'll leave us alone, then, if you please," said Tori bravely. "Unless you want to fight off all five of us, plus the tiger."

"Are all five as big as you?" the tall man asked dryly. "If so, I'll take my chances."

Bailey reached inside his coat for the claw, his only weapon, and looked back to check on the others. Hal, Gwen, and Phi peered up at him from the shadows of the tunnel, unsure of what to do.

The tall man walked toward them, keeping his eyes on Tori.

"You're awful brazen for such a skinny bit of lass," he said. "I know some traders that'd have a fine time whipping that gall right out of you."

Tori's lips became pinched, and her eyes narrowed.

"I *did* mention the tiger, right?" she said sharply.

Then two things happened all at once: the tall man moved forward so quickly that Tori hardly had a chance to defend herself. He grabbed her wrists and ignored the snakes that slithered onto his hands, attempting to frighten him off. At the same time, the short man lifted a small tube to his lips. He blew, and a dart swished through the air and sank into Taleth's neck.

"No!" shouted Bailey as he frantically tried to keep his eyes on the tall man, the short man, and Taleth. Taleth, who had begun to advance on the tall man, now stumbled to one side. Hal, Gwen, and Phi rushed up from the tunnel, shouting. Hal ran to Tori, and the girls to Taleth as she fell, one paw twitching.

"Yes, I believe you *did* mention the tiger," said the tall man. He now held Tori to him, pressing a short, fat knife to her throat. Hal stood back, frozen. "Now, the rest of you," he said, eyeing each of them where they stood paralyzed by shock. "You'll let Edder here tie you up, and you won't give us any fuss, or you'll be saying some sad good-byes."

"Don't hurt her," Hal cried.

"What did you do to Taleth?" Bailey demanded, although the fuzziness in his own head, clouding his vision and urging him to sleep, told him almost all he needed to know. The short man, Edder, walked toward the tiger and the other girls with coils of rope hoisted onto his thick shoulder.

"That's the furry one, I take it?" croaked Edder. "Just a sleepy-bit." He pulled the dart out of her neck, and Bailey saw a spot of blood staining her white fur. He wanted nothing more than to lie down next to her and close his eyes. His feet and hands weighed on him like anvils.

"She's alive," said Gwen, her hands on Taleth's flank.

"I know," Bailey murmured. Then he sank to his knees. Edder tied Taleth's paws, then tied Hal's and the girls' hands behind them before moving on to Bailey.

"I think I guessed which one is the tiger's kin," he said to the tall man, laughing as he lifted Bailey's groggy head to get a better look at him.

"Your breath stinks," Bailey said, but his voice seemed to float away from him, the words dancing in the air. He shook his head, willing himself to focus. "Like rotten cactus..."

"You little *ant*," said Edder, sounding very far away. "What do you think, Micah? Should we *crush* him like an ant?"

"No. Dominae's paying a saucy snailback to get all the Trent Melore supporters rounded up," said Micah, the tall man. "But I wager the tiger here is the *real* prize. Any fool can claim to be a prince, but there's no mistaking a white tiger! What I wouldn't give to be the man delivering that pelt to the palace. Viviana'd get weak in the knees and crown me *king*, I bet."

"Even better we've got this lot, since I heard the *real* Trent is captured and being held in a Dominae prison," said Edder. "Soon they won't be caring about the Allies no more."

"That don't mean anything," said Micah, standing over Bailey. "Even if there is a tiger, and it really *did* show up at the Fair. The true Trent Melore would've been smart enough not to show his face in front of Viviana. Bloodthirsty, that woman. But the tiger will be a treat she'll be happy to see."

Bailey's hands shook in their bonds, and his head swam. He tried to focus—these men claimed that Tremelo was captured. Had things gone so terribly wrong since they'd left the Dark Woods? At least there, they'd had the protection of the RATS, and could have helped to fight if the Dominae had found them. At least there, he wasn't, once again, risking his friends' lives in a place where no one would find them.

Micah turned to Bailey. He seemed about to drawl another threat—but as soon as his mouth parted to speak, Bailey saw something flash from the corner of his eye—he heard a thud, and the man stumbled backward with a knife buried up to the hilt in his chest. Tori screamed. The man's eyes went wide, confused, and then he fell back into the sand. Edder took no time at all in running the opposite direction.

Bailey turned. What he saw made his jaw drop.

A woman, so tan and sunburned it was impossible to tell what color her skin had been at birth, stood facing them, her throwing arm still extended. She wore a blue scarf tied over an abundance of reddish-brown curls, and dirt-stained men's pants tucked into a pair of laced boots, out the top of which Bailey could see at least two more knife hilts nestled.

Behind her was a fleet of ships—at least, that's what they looked like. White sails, nearly twenty of them, billowing in the desert breeze. Bailey squinted his eyes against the hot sun. The hulls of the ships were hooked onto the rails of the old rigi tracks. They glided slowly, pulled by the wind in their powerful sails.

Phi gasped.

"It's true—you *are* real," Phi said, smiling.

"Who are they?" asked Tori.

"I apologize if I startled you," said the woman. "Perhaps *welcome* isn't the right word, as in our settlement we move where we please, instead of staying in one place. But welcome is what you are, if you're in need of help. We are the town of Defiance."

Eight

THE IMPOSING WOMAN STRODE past Bailey and his friends, knelt, and retrieved her knife from the dead smuggler's chest. After wiping it on her pant leg, she cut the ropes binding the girls' hands, then Hal's, and finally Bailey's, before returning the knife to her left boot. Two long-eared jackrabbits hopped over to play in the sand next to her. Bailey immediately stood, still wobbly, and stumbled over to Taleth. Her heavy eyelids began to flicker.

"Tell me," said the strange woman, "what a group of children are doing wandering the eastern Plains on their own."

Bailey glanced around at his friends, as though any of them might know exactly how to address a strange woman from a desert ship who'd just killed a man right in front of them. He realized how very dry his mouth was.

Phi stood up and stepped forward.

"We're traveling to the Bay of Braour," she said.

The woman settled her eyes on Taleth, who opened her own. Taleth rolled into a sitting position and shook her heavy head. Bailey felt the cloudiness begin to lift from his own mind, and he wrapped his arms around her neck.

"Traveling to Braour, in the company of a legendary beast," the woman said, looking at Taleth, not with awe but with deep respect. Bailey had the sense that this person never showed surprise, no matter what. "I look forward to hearing more." She smiled. "My name is Annika. Come, I'll show you where you can wash the dust off of you."

Taleth emanated a pleasant energy. Unlike before, she felt comfortable, happy even, in the presence of this woman. Bailey knew they could trust Annika. They stood and followed her lead as she led them to the strange, rail-riding ships.

Defiance was like no "place" Bailey had ever seen before. The land ships were cobbled together with what looked like scrap wood and metal. In addition to sails, they sported chimneys and windows, doors and steps, like moving cabins. He saw heavy-bolted wheels connecting the ships to the rigi tracks, but tucked into the undercarriages of the ships were wooden wheels as well.

"Do those lower?" he asked, pointing to heavy levers adjacent to the extra wheels. "Can you sail on the sand, too?"

Annika nodded. "We need to be able to move in order to protect ourselves, and others."

She led them from ship to ship, showing them where the citizens of Defiance kept their collective food, met for council, stored weapons, and slept. As they passed, faces peered at them from the decks and windows of the strange caravan, staring especially at Taleth. All of the faces were female. Jackrabbits hopped out of one structure and scampered alongside Annika. She was clearly Animas Jackrabbit, which made Bailey think of his dad, Animas Rabbit. When he finally saw his mom and dad again, he knew he'd have trouble describing the strange place he found himself in now.

"You're all women," said Gwen.

"Many of us were slaves," Annika said. "And some are here after escaping their families. We're safer out here together." She seemed to Bailey to be the obvious leader, but she claimed that there was no such person in Defiance. "All of us are in charge of our own lives here—for many, it's the first time that that has been so. The Dust Plains are very cruel, especially for women. Which is why I did what I did back there, by the canyon."

She stopped and looked pointedly at Tori. "Those men you were speaking with are known slave traders. And nothing fetches as high a price out here as a young, strong girl." Tori swallowed, and opened her mouth as if to say thank you. But the words must have seemed insignificant, for she said nothing.

Annika touched Tori's shoulder, indicating that she understood, and then she reached into her pants pocket and removed a brass pocket watch. She flipped it open and showed it to them.

"My mother's," Annika said. "She lived her entire life in slavery, traded from camp to camp in the Plains. She died trying to escape—but many other women with her managed to make it out, including me. We vowed never to let it happen to us again. Some wanted revenge." She shook her head. "But that's no way to live, either. We just want safety. And here, we have it."

She led them to an area where some women were busy setting up a table made from long planks of wood and an old door laid on some sawhorses. Others tied a fabric canopy to tall posts to keep the dust away. Annika gestured to a set of barrels strapped to the nearest ship.

"Our water," she said. "Use it sparingly, if you please."

Bailey and the others washed their faces and arms with water from metal taps stuck into the sides of the barrels, taking care not to spill too much on the dry ground. The water felt so cool and good on Bailey's skin. He tried not to think too hard about how long it had been since he'd had a proper bath.

When he entered the tent with Taleth, he found that a whole group of women and even some kids had gathered around the table to eat with him and his friends. They whispered and gasped as Taleth padded in, not as adept as Annika at containing their surprise. Bailey caught the eye of one woman with silver-and-black-streaked hair already sitting at the table. She smiled widely and nodded in deference to him, as though she knew him. Next to her stood a little boy with Annika's same tan skin and reddish hair.

"You can call me the Tully," the woman said. "And this is Lukas, our son." Annika sat down next to the Tully and squeezed her arm. The boy, Lukas, hid behind Annika and poked his head out only slightly. Bailey guessed he was six or seven.

"Sit," said Annika, indicating a wide-open spot at the table for them. Bowls of fruit and plates of chickpea mash and cactus blossom were brought out along with loaves of warm bread. The citizens of Defiance sat around the table or leaned against the tent poles, warily watching Bailey and his friends eat. Annika bit into a cactus blossom.

"So tell me—in more detail, perhaps—why it is that you're traveling to Braour," she said.

Bailey locked eyes with Hal, who chewed slowly on a piece of melon. He trusted Annika—at least, he wanted to. But were they wise to be speaking so openly in front of the whole camp? He wondered what Tremelo would think.

Phi nudged Gwen to speak.

"Because it was fated," she said.

"Fated?" asked the Tully. She smiled, revealing a large gap between two of her right upper teeth. "One look at your tiger and I'd almost believe that."

"We're building an army," said Phi.

Bailey felt his cheeks growing hot.

"An army against whom?" asked Annika. She drew her shoulders back defensively. "Who would ask children to fight for them?"

"We're fighting against Viviana Melore and the Dominae," Bailey said. He saw a flicker of recognition in Annika's eyes. "She can control animals' wills, and has already done terrible things with Dominance. She'd lead an army of people's own kin against them. The Animas bond would mean nothing. It would destroy the kingdom."

Annika's dark-red eyebrows rose, but her face remained calm.

"The kingdom's destruction has little to do with us," she said. "The powers of Aldermere didn't help us when we were enslaved to traders, or beaten by our husbands and brothers. You say Viviana Melore is behind this movement?"

Bailey nodded.

"Then you should know whom you're speaking to—I wouldn't be alive and free if it were not for her." She stood, and her hand reached deep in her pocket to pull out the brass pocket watch once more. Her thumb moved over the ornate engraving; the gesture seemed familiar and full of emotion. "My mother may have died that day, but it was Viviana who helped the rest of us escape."

"But she's not like you." Gwen spoke from the other end of the table, cautiously. The eyes of all the women listening turned to her. "You said you're interested in safety, not revenge—Viviana wants revenge, but not against one person. She wants to destroy an entire kingdom that failed her. An entire world. She wants to enslave it, as it did to her. No one would be safe. Not even you."

Annika lowered her scarf. Her dark-auburn hair tumbled down around her shoulders as she studied each of them in turn.

"I wonder if you know just how large a task you're taking on. An army? You won't find loyal soldiers out here—there are too many people out for themselves. Or who believe, as we do, that we owe Aldermere nothing."

"But we have to try," said Bailey. "And if enough people follow us, then we can make Aldermere *better*, not just safe. You'd be fighting for the True King, and he wouldn't forget that."

"Another king," scoffed Annika. "One's just the same as the next, if you ask me."

"That's not true—" began Tori, but Annika cut her off.

"We'll help you get closer to the Bay, though I have doubts about this army of yours," she said. "You can stay the night. No one will harm you while you're under our protection."

"Thank you," said Bailey. He was relieved that Annika would let them stay, but he felt a strange shudder when he thought of Annika's gratitude toward Viviana. Ever since he'd learned what Dominance was, he assumed that only humans with hearts as dark as Viviana's own could feel anything but disgust and pity toward her. But he was wrong.

"We are headed across the canyon tomorrow," Annika continued. "You may ride with us if you like."

"Across?" said Hal. "How? The rigi tracks don't go that far."

"With difficulty," Annika answered. "Ours is a dangerous passage. And the kingdom you are so eager to defend has never done anything to help ease that journey—or to stop the reason we choose to go. We cross the canyon because it's the only way we can bring others who have escaped the traders to safety. We make the trip as often as we can. If Aldermere wished, it could repair the tracks, or build a bridge. But we fend for ourselves, and we do well enough."

"Why not travel farther east, where the canyon ends?" Tori asked. "I'd rather do that than plunge to my death. Seems obvious."

"Where the canyon ends in the east is where the Otherlands begin," said the Tully. She leaned her elbows onto the table. Her eyes lit up with the enjoyment of telling a good story. "And no one goes there. Impassible rocks, dust, and caverns. Only know one woman ever ventured to the Otherlands and lived, and to do it, she had to turn into her own kin. No one could survive as a human out there."

"She *became* her kin?" Phi said. "How?"

The Tully shook her head.

"Hard choice, that. I tried to talk her out of it. But in the end, I was overpowered."

Hal and Tori glanced at each other, clearly skeptical. Gwen tightened her sweater around herself as if she were cold. When Bailey met her eye she looked away quickly.

"She's telling the truth," said Lukas, who had been watching all five of them, and Taleth, since they'd entered the tent. "Mam can do all kinds of things like that."

The Tully patted his arm.

"That's enough, my little lizard," she said.

The conversation faded as Bailey and his friends tucked into their meals, enjoying the food that was so much more satisfying than the dried fruit Digby had been able to smuggle to them in the tunnels. Phi and Tori were sitting next to each other, and Bailey figured they'd made up—if he could even call it that, since they hadn't fought in the tunnels so much as vented to each other. Looking at them, he got the sense that Tori was still all right. Smiling, laughing, comfortable in her skin. Hal, too, looked in his element as he discussed the auditory benefits of the tunnels with a woman who was also Animas Bat. But Gwen seemed distant still, while Phi picked lightly at her food and stared—until she caught Bailey looking—at the Tully.

After the meal, the women of Defiance prepared their fleet for the next day's journey. Bailey and the others helped to repair holes in the ships' sails and replace frayed ropes. As he worked, Bailey could not stop thinking about Annika's assertion that the kingdom did not deserve her help, as well as her past with Viviana. Out here in the Dust Plains, things like loyalty and allegiance were not as easy to grasp as he had once thought. He hoped that when he found the army the Loon's book had spoken of, they would be easier to convince.

At the end of the day, Annika took them to a ship lined with narrow cabin berths. She dug around in a trunk for some extra bedrolls and carried them up to the exposed upper deck for Bailey, Hal, and the girls. Around the ship, women sat talking in low voices at flickering campfires. Above, a thousand stars looked down. Bailey settled in and tried to sleep, but his eyes stayed open, and his mind active. One by one his friends' breathing became slower and deeper. Hal began to snore.

Taleth hadn't followed them onto the ship. Wide-awake, she had padded off to take in the night. Without her by his side, Bailey didn't feel entirely safe. He rose and climbed down a thick rope ladder that hung on the side of the ship, and searched for Taleth in the light of the campfires. She sat a ways from the camp, looking out over the canyon that they would cross in the morning. Her fur shone pale blue in the evening light. She turned to watch him approach, and as her eyes met his, he suddenly felt sad. She was so beautiful and powerful, but she was the only one left of her kind. The world seemed to him to be growing darker and darker. It was more full of evil, as well as things *like* evil, but not so easy to understand: neglect, hurt, vengeance. Taleth was beautiful and good, but when she was gone, the white tigers would be gone forever. Like King Melore, or the Elder, who both would have fought against Dominance willingly, if they'd known how.

Bailey sat down a few feet from the edge of the canyon and looked up—he could see constellations like Nature's Twins and the Backward-Facing Otter. Off in the distance, unseen, lay the mysterious Otherlands that the Tully had spoken of. He leaned against Taleth and felt calmed by the steady rhythm of her breathing. The kingdom was so much larger than he'd ever known, in so many ways. He felt a deep stirring within him, and that was the moment when Taleth roared.

He felt a feeling building in his chest and lungs—his own noise—that had to come out. He opened his mouth and let out a loud, guttural yell, which he heard echoed back to him across the canyon, again and again, growing even louder until it faded like the dying sun. Taleth roared again. Their two noises mixed together and echoed back to them. Bailey smiled. He still felt confused, and the vastness of the Plains around him still felt undeniably empty, but that sound of defiance, multiplied, gave him hope.

Nine

TREMELO'S CAPTOR HAD NOT spoken for two days—not once. The bag around Tremelo's head made it impossible for him to see, and now, with the sun setting, sound was all he could rely on to give him any clues as to where he was and who had taken him. The kidnapper had tied a rope around both his wrists with some slack length between them, giving Tremelo a small range of movement. But that rope was tied to another, by which his captor led him over the craggy rocks and boulders of the Peaks. The air was thinner here, and colder.

He'd thought about escape, but then what? Run blindly into the mountains? He had no way of knowing which direction to go, or who might be waiting for him. He could sense, too, that many animals prowled along the mountain paths nearby. He heard the snaps of twigs and branches against their hides; he could smell the mineral stench of fresh carnivorous kills. The foxes of these woods lived in fear of predators that could easily overpower them. If he ran, he had no knowing whether these animals would avoid him or seek him as prey.

The rope around his hands slackened, and he heard the person who had been leading him through the Peaks busy himself with making a fire. They had stopped to make camp.

"I'd like to sit, please," Tremelo said. He heard footsteps and felt a hand on his chest guiding him backward.

"Behind you," a voice said.

Tremelo kicked behind him and felt what seemed to be a fallen log. He eased himself down, sighing with relief. His knees and feet were on fire with pain.

"So you do speak," he said. "Any chance you'll tell me where we're going?"

All that answered him was the crackling of dried leaves in the newly made fire.

"Not that this little stroll through the mountains isn't a pleasure," Tremelo mumbled.

All was silence until a few minutes later, when the mysterious person crouched close and lifted the bag over Tremelo's head just high enough to hold a spoon of warm food up to Tremelo's mouth. As Tremelo slurped what tasted like turnip mush, he counted himself lucky that at least he was being fed. He'd have given almost anything for the bag to be taken all the way off, however. It had become greasy with neck-sweat, and he could smell his own breath inside it.

He swallowed the last bits of his meager meal and, trying his best to sound cavalier and unconcerned, attempted conversation once more.

"I don't suppose you'll tell me who you are," he said.

"Don't matter who I am," said the man who'd been leading Tremelo in silence for two days. Although he mumbled, his words might as well have been shouted, they were such a shock to Tremelo's ears. "Matters more who *you* are."

"Is that so?" Tremelo answered. His left arm itched, but there was nothing he could do with his arms behind his back. "And just who do you think I am?"

"Not going to play that game," said the man. "We both know who you are, and what it means."

The man yanked on the rope, pulling Tremelo up off of the log. He was led a few paces away, where the man went about tying the rope to a tree.

"Can I look forward to some more lively talk, when we reach our destination, at least?" Tremelo asked. "You haven't even made a direct threat on my life yet, and I love those."

"I'm taking you to the queen," came a gruff reply. "That threat enough for you?"

Tremelo almost wished he hadn't asked. Of course, it had been a possibility he'd considered, but to hear it said out loud made him shudder: he was being taking to Viviana. He'd thought—why, he didn't know—that he'd have more time before it came to this. She would almost certainly kill him. And then, without even a thought, she'd continue her plan to drive Aldermere into complete darkness. Animals would be turned, in essence, into machines. Humans would feel bereft without their kin, and then, as humans do, they'd adapt. They'd become cold and uncaring. Would it take generations, he wondered, for Aldermere to forget that it had ever had something so precious as the Animas bond? Or merely a few years under Viviana's rule? Would the fighting continue without him? He imagined the RATS and the Velyn losing hope. Even Bailey, the child whose spirit seemed unquenchable, could not be asked to carry on without him. Instead of saving the kingdom, he'd merely be a blot of ink in the history books that would chronicle Viviana's terrible reign.

The man finished tying the ropes.

"Get some sleep, Trent Melore," he said.

"Not likely," Tremelo whispered to himself. He leaned his head back against the bark of the tree. His elbows bent at an uncomfortable angle, and the ground underneath him was littered with sharp sticks. But he knew it wasn't the physical conditions that would make sleep impossible. Instead, it would be the terrible, dark thought that now played through his mind like an ominous song: *Even kings can die.*

Ten

GWEN THOUGHT FOR A moment that the tiger's echoing roar was a part of her dream: she'd been lost in the Dark Woods, unnerved by the closeness of large animals just out of sight in the trees. But when she opened her eyes, the roar still echoed. She sprang up and ran to the railing of the ship's deck. But Bailey and Taleth were safe, sitting peacefully together at the canyon's edge. Gwen breathed deeply and allowed her heartbeat to return to its normal rhythm. Phi stirred in her blankets.

"What's wrong?" Phi asked. She sat up, her eyes barely open.

"Nothing," said Gwen. "Everything's fine."

Phi pulled the blanket up over her shoulders and stood up to join Gwen at the railing, rubbing her eyes. "You're a bad liar."

"I'm just anxious. When I was traveling to Fairmount from the Gray I used to play that harmonica when I couldn't sleep."

Phi nodded, freeing up the blanket so Gwen could huddle under it too. "Maybe you could hum some of the tunes?"

Gwen tried a few bars she'd remembered learning. She was suddenly filled with a sadness and nostalgia for the Elder, her old mentor. She'd lost him and her bond with the owls, one tragedy on the heels of another. "The only thing I've gained out of all of this is uncertain visions."

"And new friends," Phi added, which made Gwen smile. Phi's company almost made her forget that the vision she'd had was of Bailey dying at their king's hand. She glanced once more at Bailey and Taleth in the distance. She wanted to go to them, but thought it best not to disturb their solitude.

"Want to take a walk?" Phi asked Gwen.

The two girls walked across the deck to look out over the strange caravan of Defiance. Below on the ground, a few campfires were still burning. Gwen straightened her cloak and climbed down from the ship. Phi followed, the blanket still wrapped around her.

Annika and the Tully sat together by the closest fire. The Tully waved when she saw Gwen approach.

"Having trouble sleeping?" the Tully asked.

"Bad dreams," Gwen answered, as a vision of Bailey flashed in her mind. Phi looked at her sideways, but didn't add anything.

Annika held out a piece of the apple she was slicing. Gwen nodded thanks, and ate it slowly. A brown jackrabbit hopped over to the fire and began scratching its long ears with its equally long back paw. Annika ran a hand through her hair, tucking it back behind her blue scarf.

"Do you really think you're going to find an army out here?" she asked the girls.

"Ani, leave them be," said the Tully.

"I don't know," Gwen answered. "But we couldn't stay where we were."

Annika sliced another piece of apple and ate it in one bite.

"Well, *that* I can understand," she said.

Gwen watched the jackrabbit until it hopped away. She was aware of the eyes of the two women watching her over the fire.

"What's your Animas?" Phi asked the Tully, perhaps hoping to ease the tension.

"Same as my name," she answered. "Animas Tullyhorn."

"I don't think I've ever heard of a tullyhorn," said Gwen, mystified. "Sorry," she added, afraid that she'd offended.

"All gone," said the Tully. "Died out when I was just a small girl. I saw one only once. Wings out to here"—she stretched her arms out wide—"and a beak like a rhino's horn. Magnificent. I changed my name to honor them when the last one died."

"What happened to them?" Phi asked, leaning forward.

The Tully shrugged. "Things die, that's life. The Plains used to be better for a lot of creatures. But Nature shifts. 'Cause of us, 'cause of time, who can tell?"

"We'll all be lucky if any of us sees our kin through another hundred years, if things keep going the way they are," Annika interjected. "Nature's shifting again, but I don't like the feel of what's going on."

"What do you mean?" Gwen asked, though she was sure she knew.

"Changes in the world around us are to be expected," said the

Tully. "But we've seen a fair amount of animals leaving their kin for the Otherlands, like they're running away from something *un*natural. The bond is hurting."

"That's exactly what we were trying to say earlier! It's all because of Viviana," Gwen said, rising to her feet. Out of the corner of her eye, she saw Annika's pocket watch glint in the firelight. "I've seen it, too, with my own kin. They're avoiding humans because of Dominance. Because of what Viviana has done."

Annika glared at Gwen.

"No one person has that much influence over the bond," she said. "I think you children are letting the powers that be in Aldermere sway you with stories. Trust me, one ruler is just like another. Nature, on the other hand, is one of a kind."

Gwen studied Annika as she stared, steel-eyed, into the fire. Annika, Gwen could tell, might not care about politics, but she cared about her world.

"You're right to be distrustful of the kingdom," Gwen went on. "I grew up in Parliament. I know what those people were like." Annika raised her eyes and looked at Gwen over the flames. Gwen pictured the Elder as she spoke—his kind eyes and his threadbare cloak manifested in her memory as though his ghost had just appeared beside her. "Some, like my mentor, were wonderful, but sad. He knew that terrible things were happening in the kingdom, but that he could never do enough to help. But so many others were schemers and locusts. No one blames you for thinking ill of them."

"Your friends do," said Annika.

"No," said Gwen. "That's where you're wrong. Our friends—Bailey, Hal, Tori—they're not fighting for what Aldermere *was*. They're fighting to save what Aldermere could become.

Tremelo—that's the king, Viviana's brother—he could remake the kingdom into someplace where there *are* no corrupt Parliament members who argue but get nothing done. He sees the bond as something that can be used to help people, which is something Parliament could never accomplish. But Viviana wants to use the bond to do to the animals exactly what those traders did to her. And to do it, she's disrupting Nature itself. It's beyond politics or who owes who. What Viviana is doing will affect the entire kingdom—you and your people included. You said it yourself. A shift is happening. You can't ignore it."

"She was a scared girl once. She showed me kindness and I'd go so far as to call us friends, once." Annika stared into the fire, and Gwen knew she was thinking of that friendship. She wondered if Annika felt for Viviana the way that she felt about Bailey, Phi, and the Elder.

"You've given us much to think about," Annika murmured after a long silence.

Gwen met the sparkling eyes of the Tully, who nodded solemnly. She knew they were done speaking to her. Rising, Gwen looked out past the rigi tracks, where the ships creaked in the night wind, to the last streaks of light across the canyon.

"Good night," Phi said to the women, standing to join her. They left Annika and the Tully gazing into the orange-blue flames of their campfire.

"You didn't tell me you had a bad dream...." Phi said.

"Yeah, not a big deal," Gwen replied. "I can't really remember it anyway."

Bailey had returned to his bed by the time they climbed back up to the ship's deck. Taleth lay curled next to him like an enormous house cat. Her tail swished and twitched in her sleep, and Gwen had the feeling that the tiger was dreaming of some sort of battle.

She and Phi lay down next to them. Phi closed her eyes and her breathing steadied within minutes, but Gwen stared up at the stars and waited for sleep.

Just before dawn, the loud crack of the unfurling sail in the wind caused Gwen to bolt awake. Annika stood on the prow of the ship, smiling down at Gwen and the others.

"It's time to make sail," she said, her voice loud with a captain's authority. "Wake up, you lubbers."

Gwen rubbed her eyes. Her friends were already awake. Phi and Tori hastily rolled up their blankets while Hal and Bailey checked their rucksacks for their supplies. Taleth was at the prow, her front paws propped up on the railing—she was sniffing the air and looked both relaxed and alert. Lukas, Annika and the Tully's son, swung overhead on a strong rope, whooping.

"Time to sail!" he shouted. "To the canyon!"

Gwen stood. Wind cascaded over the deck, sending whirls of sand into the air.

"We'll make good time to the pass," said Annika. "As long as we get moving while the wind is strong and in our favor."

The line of landships behind Annika's creaked in the wind as sail after sail unfurled and snapped. The decks were crowded with women and children pulling and fastening ropes. Gwen pulled her cloak around her to guard against the sandy wind. Annika, seeming not to care, let her scarf whip about her head; her focus was on the southern horizon.

As one, the sails filled, and the ships of Defiance surged into motion. The deck swayed and bucked at first, and the boards under Gwen's feet shuddered. But after a moment, it was as though the heavy hull had caught up with the urging energy of the wind, and the ship glided along the rigi tracks. They were traveling at the canyon's edge. Its red rock looked like a ribbon across the dry brown sand. Gwen watched the desert slide past them from the railing of the deck. Phi and Bailey joined her there, while Hal and Tori stood at the prow. Bailey climbed up on the railing to get a better look, and stood a foot above all of them. Gwen resisted the urge to grab his shirt and pull him back down. He looked thrilled. Taleth padded up next to him and rubbed her neck on his legs. A funny sight, since she was enormous.

Lukas, done with swinging, jumped down onto the deck.

"I love fording the pass," he said. "Mom and Mam hate it."

"How come?" Bailey asked. He sounded excited, while Gwen felt terrified.

"What happens?" she asked him.

Lukas scratched his brown, wavy hair and had the look of a child who was trying not to smile.

"I guess you'll see," he said. He pointed out toward the canyon. "We can't do it here. Too wide. Too dangerous. We go a bit north, where the canyon gets narrower. But it's still deep!"

Bailey, Tori, and Hal joined them. Hal clutched the railing; his face was drained of color.

"I think I'm getting seasick," he groaned.

"We're not even at sea!" Bailey said.

"Yeah, we're not even at sea!" Lukas repeated. He looked up at

Bailey, pleased to see him laughing. All the while, Hal closed his eyes tightly and shook his head.

The fleet sailed several miles along the deserted track; after an hour, Gwen had become accustomed to the gentle rocking of the ships as the sails carried them onward. But then Annika sent up another shout:

"Detatch!"

The word echoed as the deputy captain of each ship down the line called out the command, and after a moment, a giant *clunk* shook the ship. Gwen heard a loud clicking noise and, along with her friends, rushed to the edge to peer over the railing. Taleth's ears perked up. Below them, six mechanical legs were unfolding from the hull of the ship—three on each side, making the ship look like a giant wooden insect. With a thud, the end of each leg landed on the ground, sending up puffs of sand. Then the legs extended, and the entire ship rose several feet in the air.

"We're not on the tracks anymore!" Phi gasped. "Look!"

"No, thank you," groaned Hal, who sat with his back against the railing.

Lukas, even more excited than he'd been earlier that morning, jumped and danced on the deck.

"We're going to the pass! We're going to the pass!" he sang. Bailey grinned ear to ear, and leaned so far forward Gwen thought she'd faint on his behalf. His squirrel kin skittering around in little gray circles, little Lukas bounced on his toes.

The ship's legs proved to be a bit unwieldy; Gwen stumbled for the railing and nearly fell when the vessel took its first step forward. Bailey caught her from behind.

"Hold on, silly!" said Lukas.

"You okay?" Bailey asked as he led her to the railing. She nodded. Sometimes it was hard to look at him without seeing him struck down, just as he was in her vision.

"Sure, sure. The view is just a little distracting," she said motioning to the canyon.

"Part of the adventure, right?" he said. She forced a smile to match his. Good, kind Bailey—as far as he knew they were making progress toward their goal of finding an army. But Gwen knew the truth: that she'd convinced them to come because they were running away. It seemed the best option at the time, but now she considered whether or not she could change the future. . . .

As the ship scuttled closer, they could now see a series of ropes spanning the width of the ravine, lodged into the rock.

"Do we cross using those?" she asked Lukas. They didn't look nearly strong enough to hold up the entire ship.

"Sure do!" he crowed. Gwen looked down at Hal. Bailey patted Hal's arm, and Taleth nudged his hip with the top of her head.

"I'm sure they know what they're doing," he said. He met Gwen's eyes, as though he was trying to reassure her too.

Gwen's fingers dug into the wooden railing as the ship creaked toward the ravine's edge.

"Descend!" shouted Annika.

The Tully unspooled a rope tied around a beam, and it swung across the front of the ship. The vessel's prow tipped downward before it stopped, perched precariously at an angle and pointed toward the deep gash in the desert. Annika hauled a rope to the edge of the prow and tossed it over one of the ropes that already spanned the canyon, creating a loop that she secured with a clamp attached to the ship's mast.

Gwen didn't want to look, but she couldn't help herself—she peered down into the canyon and immediately felt dizzy. She couldn't even see the bottom, only the thin patterns of rock formations as they grew closer together on their way down, obscuring the true depth of the canyon. Her vision telescoped and blurred.

"Prepare the cannons!" Annika yelled.

"Cannons?" Phi whispered.

"Okay, everyone," Lukas announced over the sound of the wind, "cover your ears!" He placed his own palms over his ears. Everyone scrambled to do the same as a blast fired.

"Again!" yelled Annika. Another woman lowered a lit torch to the cannon's back end, and everyone on deck braced themselves. It thundered again, and Gwen watched, aghast, as a rope attached to a metal harpoon was shot across the canyon. The harpoon sank into the red rock on the other side, accompanied by a shower of displaced stones. The blasts were echoed all along the edge of the ravine; the other ships were lined along the canyon, each firing their own ropes across the chasm.

"Lock them!" commanded Annika. Her shout was repeated down the line, and the women on each deck ran to secure the ends of the ropes to metal clasps attached to the front of the ship.

Lukas leaned out over the railing next to Bailey, watching as the ropes were tied down.

"Any minute now!" he said.

"Surely the ship can't be supported by just a few ropes?!" Gwen asked. Her heart had begun beating wildly; she imagined the ropes snapping with the pressure of so much weight.

"Mom said those are just in case," Lukas said, grinning. "You might all want to hold on, though."

Gwen and her friends took his advice without a word and braced for whatever would come next. At the prow, Annika clutched a rope and raised her other arm high.

"Release!" she shouted.

Gwen couldn't help but scream as the ship tipped forward off the rock. The slack ropes hanging from the line grew taut, but not before the entire ship shuddered, and a pair of sails unfurled not from the mast, but from the sides of the hull.

"Wings!" shouted Phi. "The ship has wings!"

"Holy Nature!" Bailey said in an awed tone. When Lukas copied him he smiled, then got serious again and shook his head. "Don't say that!"

The canvas caught the air and the white sail billowed. The ship seemed to float as it swung forward on the line. Annika and her crew tugged on the ropes that had been harpooned into the canyon, leading the flying ship across.

Gwen gaped at the sight of the many ships sailing across the canyon, all in a line crisscrossed with ropes and dotted with the blinding-white sails in the late morning sun.

"It's beautiful," she said.

"Just don't look down," answered Hal.

She did the exact opposite. As the wind blew through Gwen's short red hair, she pushed it away from her face and looked down. From here the canyon was narrower, but much, much deeper. The bottom looked like a line the thickness of a spider's floss.

This high up, the wind made everything chilly. She leaned into Phi and together they peered into the canyon, or tried to. Taleth wedged herself between them, and Gwen drew comfort from her heaving breath and the feel of her thick white fur.

Below were so many shades of orange and red—an incredible blend of smooth stone and jagged cliffs. She'd never felt more terrified or awestruck. Nature had made this. It had made all of them.

"Hal!" Tori exclaimed, grabbing his arm. "You *have* to look!"

Hal clutched her hand as he turned, his eyes still clenched tightly. When he opened his eyes, he closed them again quickly. "Okay, I did it—I looked!"

They'd passed the deepest part of the canyon, and the other side seemed within reach—growing larger as they approached.

"Will the line hold?" Gwen asked Lukas.

He shrugged. "It has every other time."

"Oh Nature," Hal groaned. "That's precisely what worries me! If these ropes haven't been replaced—"

"*Shhhhhh*," Tori interrupted. "We'll find out soon enough, won't we?"

Bailey hopped off the rail and went to stand by Annika's side, his eyes gleaming with excitement. He was transfixed on the anchors. Lukas, of course, followed him excitedly and scooped a squirrel up when it scurried toward his feet. Taleth pushed off the railing by Gwen and Phi to pace behind them.

"It's almost like we're flying, isn't it?" Phi asked. She didn't seem nearly as scared as Gwen was. The two girls stumbled as the whole ship tipped back dramatically the last part of the way. The crew widened their stances as they collected the ropes, going about their work like this was normal—to sail over a canyon. The ship strained and stuttered the last bit of the way. Gwen held on fiercely to the railing with one hand and to Phi's arm with the other.

Eleven

BAILEY WATCHED THE ROCK crumble away from where the anchor dug in, nervous and exhilarated all at once. Taleth nudged her nose to his hand, and suddenly, he couldn't see himself anymore—or the canyon, either. The wide, unadorned plains closed in and became blackish-green trees, and the sky overhead changed from bright blue to hazy, snow-tinged gray. But he could still feel the wind blowing over the canyon, and he could hear Hal complaining.

Bailey knew, without understanding exactly how or why, that he was seeing Taleth's memories. She hurried over mossy rocks and nettle-strewn paths, surrounded by piney mountain trees. Her ears pricked—she heard a cry, the wail of a human infant.

Bailey's eyes snapped open. He was gripping the cable rails, white knuckled from the intense effort. Even in Taleth's mind, he hadn't let go. He felt the power of their connection flowing through him, filling his chest and lungs and mind with energy that rippled out from him—if he looked down, he thought, he might even be able to see it, the energy felt so real and tangible.

Then the ship lifted the last part of the way and landed with a thud. He saw Gwen and Phi sink to the deck.

"Excellent, crew!" Annika yelled. She walked down the center of the ship. It was silent apart from the heavy steps of her boots.

The kids followed the crew off the ship, with Taleth going first. She made sure to stay low and swayed her tail back and forth as she looked to either side. Her big, blue eyes took in the new scenery, and Bailey felt a sense of excitement and caution. He nudged her from behind, and she purred as she hurried along.

They walked along a canyon switchback, passing all the different landing sites for the other ships that had crossed with them. Women and children on the crew were scattered ahead and behind Bailey's group. Eventually, the path led to rough steps carved into the cliffside, and patches of thick, reedy grass gave way to thicker vegetation. Bailey and Annika took the lead, with Taleth stalking alongside them with a nervous energy. Behind them, Lukas pointed out all of the flora in their Latin names, which seemed of genuine interest to Tori and Hal.

Snakes slithered in and out of cracks at the very edge of the canyon, attempting to get Tori's attention—but now she and Hal were fighting over a Latin derivative. At the very back were Phi, Gwen, and the Tully, who talked quietly as they gazed into the canyon.

Two jackrabbits scurried about the grass alongside their party, at first wary of Taleth, who gave a low growl. Annika called the hares forward several times, and even offered sun-dried vegetables from her satchel. But still they wouldn't come. She glanced over to Bailey, and he took it as a sign to pull Taleth back.

"Give them some room, girl," Bailey called, and Taleth moved to Bailey's far side, albeit reluctantly.

"Is she okay?" Annika asked. "And are *you* okay?"

Bailey nodded. "Yeah. It's just that everything is so new. . . ."

He felt exhilarated—like they were finally onto something. But he was scared, too, and not just of what lay beyond the canyon. He was worried about the fate of the kingdom. Could they really find an entire army to fight for Tremelo? If good people like Annika and the Tully wouldn't fight for him, then who would?

"There's much of the world I haven't seen, either," she said as the jackrabbits hopped behind her. "Your Gray City for instance."

"It's nice but a bit dirty," Bailey admitted. "I'm from the Lowlands, myself."

She nodded. "I would've guessed. You seem like you're used to hard work."

Bailey grinned, and ran his hand through his short blond hair. He stood a little straighter, and would've loved to enjoy the compliment if it hadn't been for Taleth. She gave a low growl behind them. When Bailey turned to look, she was edging one of the rabbits away toward the grass. He moved closer to her, shooing her off the rabbits.

"Nature!" Annika exclaimed, shaking her wrist in the air. One of the jackrabbits had bitten into her finger. "That's never happened before. . . ."

"Annika!" one of the women ahead called. Without pause, Annika broke into a sprint up the remainder of the path. Bailey followed, dodging and weaving through the scattered women and children. Taleth clawed her way up the side of the mountain and met them there.

A dozen people cowered in the center of just as many desert animals, all Dominated, by the vacant look in their eyes. There was a village here once, that much was obvious. There was shredded canvas that looked like the Defiance sails and wooden structures that had made the walls of homes. Bits and pieces of a life were scattered—pans, clothes, broken ceramics. A woman stood on the edge, her light hair wrapped in a colorful scarf. She was cradling a baby, bouncing it the way mothers do when they're trying to distract them.

"No," Annika whispered under her breath. The Tully came running up, huffing and puffing.

"Myra, are you alright?" the Tully called out.

"We tried to send word, but we failed," the woman with the scarf called back. "We don't know—"

She was cut off by the hiss of a brown desert fox, and she cowered. Bailey only now realized the people were covered in scratches and bite marks, their clothes shredded. And that there were two men on either side of the circle, standing tall with smug looks on their faces.

"Asked you to be quiet, didn't I?" the one on the left said, speaking in a thick, clipped accent as they did in the industrial district of the Gray.

"MAM, MOM!" Lukas cried from behind. A squirrel had bitten into his arm and wouldn't let go. Lukas swung him around wildly, but the animal was clamped on tight. Bailey ran to his side and grabbed it by the tail. The squirrel let go instantly and swung himself up on Bailey's arm, then jumped down and hid behind a low shrub. It seemed suddenly ashamed.

Back where he stood, a commotion had broken out, with Annika's jackrabbits lunging at her and the Tully. She yelled for them to stop. "What is this madness?" she asked.

Bailey realized they'd only started attacking once he'd left her side. It was the orbs in his pocket—the ones he'd taken from Tremelo's office. He pulled them out of his pocket and felt the metal heat in his hands.

"It's an antidote!" he said out loud.

"A what?" Phi asked.

Bailey looked up at his friends, and at the terrified faces of the people of Defiance. Most of them were watching Annika or struggling with their own kin who'd accompanied them on the ship.

"It's something Tremelo was developing. An antidote to Dominance!" He showed the three orbs in his hands. "We're going to have to toss them back and forth to get to the men."

"Do *what*?" Hal asked. He looked up at two bats circling, and moved in closer toward Bailey.

"Just do as I say, everyone. Phi, you take the left side and I'll pass it to you. We'll go back and forth to stay safe. Tori, Gwen, are either of you decent at Scavage? It's just like tossing a Flick—"

"I know how to catch a ball," Tori interrupted. "How about you, Parliament?" she asked Gwen, but her tone was kind. Gwen nodded so forcefully that red curls tumbled down the front of her face.

"Just toss it back and forth, keep moving, watch your partner's back, and throw them the orb if they look like they're in trouble. We need to get Annika to the center where she can help handle the men." He went over a loose plan of who should go where.

"And what am I supposed to do?" Hal asked.

"Hold on to the third and stay close to me," Tori answered. She and Hal each grabbed an orb from Bailey's hand. "On your count, Bailey."

He nodded. "One, two, THREE." The kids went sprinting in different directions. Bailey grabbed Annika's arm and tried to pull her forward. At first she refused, even as the jackrabbits fell away and calmed.

"I have no kin," the Tully said. "I'll take care of Lukas. GO."

And so Bailey, Taleth, and Annika ran side by side. Taleth pawed down an armadillo who attacked along the way, and all the while Bailey watched Phi—who was quick on her feet and knew when to duck and roll to evade some animal or another. But he saw that Carin was swooping down and called out. He released the orb just as she looked up, and she caught it as Carin was mid-dive. The falcon pulled up abruptly and clawed at the fox who'd been charging toward her.

Gwen and Tori held their own, though they stayed closer to each other and handed off the orb—every so often coming back together again to trade. Hal stayed close behind, and his bats proved useful, flapping around a vulture in order to disorient it.

A dingo charged at them, and Annika raised her forearm so the dog bit onto it first.

"Bailey!" Phi called, throwing him the orb. The dingo fell away, and Taleth batted it to the side with her massive head.

The two men, who'd been so smug earlier, seemed scared as Annika and Bailey gained ground. They sent more animals toward them, but they all fell away once they got close enough, scared and unwilling now that the power of Dominance had left them. The men must have been well practiced—Bailey didn't know of anyone who could control kin other than their own, besides Sucrette and Viviana herself. Annika crouched down and pulled a blade out of her boot. She threw it at one man's shoulder and he went down, and all the other animals near him seemed to fall out of his spell. The pain must've destroyed his concentration.

A loud screech sounded across the way, and Phi screamed. Bailey looked up just as she brought her arms to her face, both Carin and the vulture nipping at her hair. Bailey launched the orb with all his strength so that it hit the vulture square on its body; it flapped and clawed, tearing through Carin's wing as it went down. There was a cascade of feathers as Phi fell to the ground and grabbed for the orb, clutching it tightly.

On Bailey's side of the commotion, the second man had broken into a sprint away from Annika, but she tackled him to the ground. He was Animas Armadillo, and the animal scurried away quickly. Myra, the woman the Tully had addressed, stood up and kicked the man in the ribs once. He let out an *oof*.

Bailey looked around, seeing that the animals had backed away. The kin that flew disappeared, apart from Carin and the bats. Carin was perched on Phi's shoulder; the girl sat with her legs crossed holding the orb to her chest. Now in the void of screams and terror there was only silence.

Annika immediately got to work, using found shreds of canvas to tie the men up. "These were the horrors you spoke of in the city? The ones Viviana Melore is responsible for?"

Bailey glanced at his friends, and they all nodded at Annika. He knew better than to keep bad-mouthing Tremelo's sister. Her work would speak for her. But he would advocate for Tremelo.

"The True King, Trent Melore, made these orbs. He's trying to undo everything Viviana has done. To bring the bond back to its purest form."

The Tully and Lukas arrived, and hugged Annika on either side.

"We'll all fight for you," Myra said.

"Yes!" Bailey exclaimed. Taleth eased against him with her flank, her tail high and relaxed. Phi smiled at him from the ground, her crown of curly brown hair shining in the sun. She pushed herself up to stand, and he was relieved to see she was okay.

"Another addition to our army!" Gwen exclaimed. "Now we can head to the Bay and pick up more would-be soldiers...."

"The Bay?" Myra asked. "There's no one at the Bay. It's desolate there, completely taken over by warlords who wield the same power as these men did." She nudged the unconscious man with her foot for good measure.

"The Domniae have taken over the Bay?" Gwen asked. Her face fell. "But the book said, 'Sunken deep at the kingdom's edge and watched by a wise and dusty army...'"

"What book do you quote, child?" the Tully said.

Everyone looked at Tori, who hesitantly pulled the book out of her beaded bag.

"I *know* that book." The Tully laughed. "The book of prophecies, correct?" She continued when she saw the surprised look on the kids' faces. "I know the Velyn well. Many of them became refugees to Defiance after the Jackal's massacre. And I know of the Seers' Glass too. And what you seek was never in the Bay at all. It's elsewhere you need to go...."

Twelve

THE CLOUD OF BLACK, glittering ash that rose above the Seers' Valley evoked memories in Viviana. It reminded her of the night the palace had burned, when she was still a girl—and again of the night, years later, when she and Annika burned down the slave trader camp and let all the girls free.

Annika. She hadn't thought of her in years, and in truth, Viviana preferred to have forgotten her old friend altogether. Viviana was the closest to the other girl when she was at her weakest. But as the soot descended from the sky, she reminded herself that she wasn't weak anymore. After all, the ash was a sign of progress. Her army was nearly complete.

She stood on the stone slab that had once held the Statue of the Twins. A piece of rubble from the statue knocked against her foot; she kicked it away. What lay before her in the valley was more majestic than any statue: a gash in the mountainside, hundreds of yards wide, spit dark ash as animal workers, Dominated to serve, hewed slab after slab of shiny, pitch-black rock from the mountain's core. The slabs were then hauled into a huge white tent, now dingy with ash, where Viviana's trained tinkerers melted and molded them into her perfect army. Soon, no upstart revolutionaries would stand a chance against her.

"Madam—one of those poachers is here to see you. He claims he has the prince."

Viviana's heart—something many doubted she still possessed—thudded with excitement. "I'll escort you to the entrance," she said, striding along the edge of the rock quarry. People toiled below, digging up soil and stone in search of her precious metal. The guard who'd summoned her, barely a man, with a hint of a mustache, walked a step behind her. With each thud of his thick boots, the thrilling anticipation building inside her grew. Trent Melore had been caught.

Since the day of the Progress Fair, she'd been imagining this moment: what she'd say to him, how he'd look, how she'd kill him. Nothing had truly prepared her for what was about to occur. Her brother. Her own, lost brother—and his life was in her hands.

She would have known him anywhere. To her followers, she'd laughed off the events at the Progress Fair as a coup staged by an imposter. If anyone asked her, she'd tell them that Trent Melore was dead, and anyone claiming to be him was a fake and a traitor.

Only she knew the truth: one look at the face of the man who'd walked onstage at the Fair, and she'd known it was him. He'd had their father's eyes.

There had been a time, many years ago, when she'd have thanked Nature that he was still alive. For all the years she was in the Dust Plains, she had dreamed of him every night. It was always the same: her running through the burning palace, only as an adult instead of a little girl. And every time she reached the nursery door, she flung it open only to find another door—and behind that door another door, and so on and so on. Trent's cries went on for hours. But finally, after hundreds of doors, she found the smoky nursery. But she hadn't found little Trent inside. She'd found little Viviana staring back at her.

"In here, my lady," said the guard. They'd arrived at the hollow space of dungeons they'd carved out of the quarry.

"Show me," she said, gesturing for the guard to lead on.

In the cell farthest from the light, she heard a shuffling and a moan. The guard hung a lantern on a hook by the cell door. Flickering light shone through the grate, casting a sinister pattern over the stone floor and the man lying prone upon it with a bag over his face. There was a second guard, taller and older, watching over him.

"Take off the mask," she said.

With a creak of the metal door, the boy-guard entered the cell and forced the wretched man to his knees. Viviana trembled. *Our father would not have wished for you to be so unkind to me*, she thought, practicing the speech she'd made to her mirror since the Progress Fair. *For this, you must be punished.*

She licked her lips without realizing it and strained forward against the bars as the guard lifted the bag off of the man's head.

"Here he is," the guard said, brandishing the bag proudly and gesturing to the man.

Viviana's heart fell. She searched this man's face but did not see her father's eyes, or the ridiculous mustache worn by her brother at the Fair. The man kneeling in the cell had a round, wide nose and eyes of muddy, indistinct brown.

"I never said I was no one!" the man yelled in an accent that placed him as a gutter ant of the Gudgeons, and not the man who'd so calmly, so nobly, spoken to her at the Progress Fair.

"You *idiot*," she said to the guard. She marched into the cell and grabbed the bag away from him. "Anyone can see this isn't the man."

"He was caught in Gribber Street, my lady, telling a crowd that he was the True King," the guard said. "Just saying it is reason enough to arrest him."

"You're wasting my time!" she shouted. All the delicious anticipation she'd felt now became fury. "There are dozens—hundreds!—of creatures like him claiming to be the True King. Will you arrest *all* of them and let the one who *dared* to threaten me go free?"

She tossed the bag at the kneeling man. It hit him in the face, and he winced.

"What should I do with him, then?" asked the guard as Viviana took her leave of the cell.

"Send him to the quarries with the rest of them," she said. "Do I need to figure everything out for you?"

As she marched out of the dungeons, the older guard called to her.

"M'lady," he said.

She spun around, furious. "And don't waste my time any further."

He flinched, just barely, and it pleased her to see it. "Of course, m'lady." He bowed his head. "There are rumors that the man you seek—the imposter from the Fair—is a professor at Fairmount."

Viviana felt a flame dance inside her chest. Of course—she remembered the boy, how even then his genius shone through in the intricate towers he'd construct from mere wooden blocks. It would make sense to pursue academia. "Then see if these rumors are true," she told the guard. "If it is so, you'll have a special place in my cabinet."

The man smiled, which irritated her. She'd done enough good deeds for the day and wished to find another victim on which to inflict her venom, so she headed toward the cluster of tents in the man-made valley of the quarry. She walked down the slope slowly, so as not to slip on loose rock. At the first tent, she yanked open the fabric flap that protected the people inside from the black soot that had gathered on everything.

"Clarke!" she called to the wretched figure huddled over a worktable. "You'll be happy to hear that the black stone is working quite well—*so* well, in fact, that I may consider feeding you this week."

In response, Clarke did not look up. "Yes, my queen," he mumbled softly. In the shadows, a metal pony with red eyes reflected the low light of the one overhead bulb.

"Exactly what I want to hear," Viviana purred. "Good work indeed."

Thirteen

TREMELO'S HANDS WERE BOUND by a strong rope, and he was tethered to a strange man. He was being held prisoner, led up a mountain and farther away from Fairmount—away from his urgent research against Dominance, and away from Fennel. The way her curious mind turned when it came upon a unique smell or an unfamiliar sound would have served him well right now. He hoped she hadn't gotten sick with worry. Tremelo needed her facilities sharp if she was to track him. Because Nature knew, his were not. He hadn't realized just how unfit he was until he had to climb up a mountainside with his hands bound, and only a sip of water through a potato sack every hour. His throat was parched, and he was dizzy from exhaustion.

"My good man, at the risk of sounding whiney I must ask: Are we there yet?" Tremelo didn't know where "there" was; his kidnapper hadn't given him much to go on.

"The queen forbids you to know anything further," he'd said, not for the first time. In fact Tremelo had counted twenty-two times at this point.

"Of course. Well, I don't suppose this bag atop my head could be removed?" Tremelo asked. It was humid with his breath. "While the people in the Gray consider themselves fashion forward, I really don't think this suits me."

"Funny," the man's gruff voice replied sarcastically.

"What's funny is your absurd devotion to your queen," he replied. "What is it, exactly, that she promised you?"

"Freedom from the bond, of course," the kidnapper said, his voice tight. Tremelo imagined him saying it through gritted teeth, and couldn't help but groan. People actually believed this drivel.

"Do not disrespect the queen," the man continued, pulling hard on the rope so that Tremelo nearly fell forward. "She said—"

But something cut through the air, a small object whistling just passed Tremelo's ear—and the rope was pulled taught before he heard the thud of something heavy hitting the ground.

Tremelo's blood froze. He stood perfectly still, terrified—wondering who was out there and what had happened. He grabbed ahold of the rope that bound him and felt his way forward until he was crouched to the ground. It led to the waist of his captor's body. He gave it a nudge. The man didn't move.

Tremelo pulled the sack off and took in a breath of fresh air for the first time in days. His captor was a thin wire of a man, unconscious—or possibly dead. When he heard footsteps behind him he felt a jolt of electro-current up his spine. The silence stretched so long that he couldn't take it anymore.

"I'll have you know I'm adept at a far-west martial art," he said, shakily. "I am well versed in pressure points and know how to kill a man in a dozen different ways." It was a bluff, of course.

Whoever was behind him gave a snort. "I hope you're not as bad a king as you are a liar," he said. The voice was familiar, gruff but friendly.

Tremelo spun around and saw none other than Eneas. "Thank Nature!" Tremelo said, standing up to shake the man's hand. "How did you find me?"

"I was tracking a group of Dominae spies up the eastern edge of the woods. I'd followed Miller into the Lowlands, but he was captured and I couldn't save him."

Tremelo sensed the hint of anger and regret in his voice. "Have you any word from the kids? Or anyone back in the tunnels? Digby?"

Eneas shook his head. "Things look bad. The tunnels were raided just after you were kidnapped. I know many of the Velyn and RATS escaped."

Tremelo was devastated to hear the news. All those people—they'd survived Viviana's Progress Fair just to be hunted like prey.

"Tremelo, the metal Miller spoke of . . . the Dominae are mining the Velyn mountains to find more of it. They're uprooting our kin."

"The metal," Tremelo repeated. He'd had a theory that it was the same metal used in the Reckoning, stitched into the heart of the metal tiger at the Progress Fair. If he was right, it was black in its raw form and silver when refined. "Do you know what they'll do with it?"

"My source doesn't know. But they will tear apart the ground upon which Aldermere stands for more and more of it. They'll mine all the way to the Underlands for all we know."

The Underlands, the place of wild, ill repute beyond the kingdom. "Impossible."

"The soil there is rich in iron ore. There have been rumors that there's division in the Dominae ranks. Some of them are still too scared to travel there, while Viviana will likely claim that as part of her kingdom too. Yet the Underlands already has a queen...."

Tremelo looked at Eneas curiously. "Another queen?" he asked. "This isn't another Velyn fairy tale, is it?"

"A fairy tale?" Eneas said, his jaw set and his eyes hard. Tremelo knew immediately he'd said the wrong thing. Eneas turned his back and began to walk up the slope. "There's still much more for you to learn, my king. A battle awaits," he called behind him.

Fourteen

"FAIRMOUNT?" GWEN ASKED IN disbelief. "But that's only a day's ride from the Gray."

"How's that the edge of the kingdom?" Hal asked.

"The prophecy . . . could we have read it wrong?" Gwen said.

She looked to Tori, who held the book open in her arms as Gwen fished the Seers' Glass out of her pocket and put it to the page. "'Sunken deep at the kingdom's edge, watched by a wise and dusty army,'" Gwen said before reading the rest. "But we can't go back to Fairmount. The whole reason we left was to escape Viviana after the Progress Fair!" Though she couldn't admit to the group that she wasn't too eager to head back in Tremelo's general direction, either. In her vision, she'd seen the True King hurt her friend, and she'd do anything in her power to stop it.

The Tully shook her head. "The book you read from is much older than any of you. A long time ago, it was Fairmount that was known to be the edge of the kingdom. It was just past the cliffs where they built it, in the very spot of woods considered to be the entrance to the Underlands."

The kids were quiet for a moment. The Underlands were rarely spoken of.

"We came all this way because I read the prophecy wrong," Phi said, breaking the silence. "This is my fault."

"This is no one's fault!" Bailey said forcefully. "If we hadn't come here we wouldn't have met Annika, the Tully, Lukas—any of these people." He pointed around at the women and children who'd been with them on the ships and been held hostage by the Dominae. "And anyway we're supposed to be raising an army, and we're sure as Nature not going to find it at school."

Lukas had stood up a little straighter at the sound of his name. "He's right!" the boy exclaimed. "Now we're part of your army."

Phi smiled a bit, and Gwen was glad Bailey had said what he did. She reached out to touch Phi's arm, but the other girl flinched and pulled back. She was about to ask what was wrong when the Tully's gentle voice pulled her attention away.

"Hold on, little lizard," the Tully said, her hand on his shoulder. "It's not so simple."

Annika's brow furrowed. She and the Tully shared a look. Myra and the others had already pledged to join their army, but the two women Gwen had come to trust most still hadn't decided.

The Tully nodded to Annika, as if the two had communicated something in that one look. "Lukas," she said, getting down on one knee, "Mum has to go with our new friends, but you and I are going to stay here."

The little boy spun around and looked up at Annika. His face had crumpled, and he looked on the verge of tears.

"I'll be back before you know it, little lizard," Annika said. She lifted the boy off the ground and hugged him close, and he somehow managed not to cry. Gwen looked away. She remembered the urgency with which she and the Elder left Parliament, the night when this all started. War was a horrible thing.

"We'll have to leave immediately," Annika said to the Tully.

Bailey looked at the rest of them. "What do you think? If we head back toward Fairmount, maybe we can find Tremelo in the tunnels?"

"No!" Gwen blurted out, though she couldn't very well tell them why. "I mean . . ." Everyone looked at her expectantly, but Gwen felt torn. She wanted to argue. She wanted the deaths to end, and if that meant keeping Bailey away from Tremelo, then she'd have to speak up. But before she could, Phi did.

"I'm staying here," her friend said. They turned to look at Phi. Carin was perched on her shoulder, and it was the first time Gwen realized how badly her wing was damaged. There was a gash through it, feathers lost around the wound and blood dripping down.

"I can carry Carin," Bailey said, a note of desperation to his voice. "We can't go without you!"

"You have to," she said as she pulled her cloak back to reveal deep gashes across her side. Claw marks. Her clothes were wet with blood, and she stumbled back—as if it had been an effort to stand straight this entire time. Tori was to her left, and caught her first. "It was while the vulture was fighting with Carin. . . ."

Gwen and Bailey rushed to either side of her, with Hal looking over their shoulders.

"Oh Nature!" Gwen whispered. "We can't leave you here by yourself!"

"She won't be by herself," the Tully said. "Lukas and I are staying, and lots of the other women and children. I have some pastes and creams that could relieve the pain and quicken the healing."

Tori grabbed Phi's hands. "I can stay," she said. Gwen remembered that they'd been roommates, and they'd spent the first part of the school year looking out for each other. Gwen suppressed a sliver of jealousy; she'd never had school friends. She'd never been in school.

"They need you," Phi said as she shook her head.

"Not as much as you do," Tori said. Gwen could see the worry behind her eyes. "Bailey is some prophesized Child of War, and Gwen is a Seer. And Hal and his bats would be good to have in the woods. They can handle this without me...."

"No," Phi said. "The fight needs you. It needs all of you. And it needs me too. When I'm better."

This sparked a series of protestations where everyone spoke over one another. Hal argued Tori's snakes would be better assets during their travel; Bailey insisted they delay their trip; Tori pointed out that she was considering studying medicine and she could be of help.

"You must trust that she knows what's best for her," the Tully said over their voices.

They all quieted then, though Gwen hadn't spoken the entire time. Her head was spinning. She didn't want to leave Phi here.

But if Bailey went to Fairmount without her, how could she protect him from her vision coming true? What if Tremelo was there, or they ran into him along the way?

"We'll respect your decision," Gwen said, her voice choked with grief. "I don't want to leave you, but the kingdom . . ."

"Go, you guys," Phi said. "Carin and I will be fine."

"Hard decisions are made in times of war," Annika said. She kissed Lukas on his dark hair and put him down. "Gather your things, everyone."

Sailing a conspicuously odd land ship back to the Lowlands did not seem, to Bailey or any of his friends, to be a good idea. Annika, thankfully, had provided transport. To help them cross the southern Plains, Myra provided them with three-wheeled contraptions, similar to motorbikes, and just as rusty and rickety as anything they might once have found in Tremelo's shop.

"I'm sorry they're not road-hardier," Myra had said when presenting them. "Or that I don't have enough for all of you." She and any other able-bodied women planned to meet them at Fairmount, after they'd had enough time to rebond with their kin.

"That's all right," said Hal. "We can share, right, Tori?"

"Only if I'm driving," Tori had said.

After two days of driving, with Taleth running alongside them, the sand dunes they passed had transformed into dry plains, and then to the snow-covered but rich earth of the farm-dotted Lowlands. They pushed on into the Dark Woods, skirting north of the mountains, and camped underneath the safety of a thorny thicket.

Gwen stared into the small fire Tori was starting, lost in her thoughts. Taleth padded behind her, brushing against Gwen affectionately as she passed—then landed with a huff on top of a bed of damp leaves nearby. Bailey arranged his coat around himself and burrowed next to his kin for warmth.

"Are you all right?" Bailey asked. It was hard for Gwen to look at him, to see the goodness of the bond at work. She wasn't sure how to answer. "I know it was hard to leave Phi behind."

Gwen ran her fingers through her hair, twisting one short lock until it was taut as a wound spring. "I miss her. I miss the owls too." She hadn't seen one owl since they left the Gray, and she missed the way their simple presence filled her heart. But it was more than that. It was the harrowing vision that flashed in her mind, and the feeling of absolute helplessness that she wouldn't be able to stop it. "Everything feels so out of control." She squeezed her eyes shut, blinking out a single tear. How could she save Bailey if she couldn't even keep herself from crying?

"Hey," he said. "We're going to put together an army. We're going to make sure Tremelo gets his kingdom back."

The king's name made her shudder. "And what if we don't?" she asked. "What if he doesn't take the throne?"

Tori looked back at her curiously. She was crouched by the fire, fanning the small flames.

"We're not going to let Viviana win!" Bailey said. He seemed like he was trying to reassure himself as much as Gwen.

She nodded in response. She couldn't keep this conversation up any longer, and she felt traitorous. Even surrounded by friends and even with the newfound knowledge that she was a Seer, she was totally adrift—orphaned again just as she was as a child wandering through the Gudgeons.

Could she change the future? She thought of Tremelo's adopted father, Thelonious Loren. They called him the Loon because he'd written down the prophecies of the Seers, because he'd *believed* them. But Gwen didn't want her own prophecies to come true. She wanted to prevent them. She wanted to fight.

The Dark Woods proved too thick to drive through quickly; they drove at a snail's pace, camping at night under the cover of low, camouflaging branches. Taleth left them for hours at a time to hunt for her own food, while Tori and Hal took charge of scavenging edible greens and winter nuts from the surrounding thickets. Hal's upbringing with his apothecary uncle had resulted in a keen eye for which plants were safe to eat, and which would cause hours of stomachaches, or worse. They slept in shifts, huddled together for warmth.

Every night, Gwen fell asleep with the Seers' Glass in her hand. She couldn't yet control her visions, but her heart ached for some sort of guidance. On the third night, the warmth of the Glass against her palm woke her up, and when she looked down she saw the spectrum of colors emanating from it. Her vision grew cloudy, then the colors swirled into one, suddenly bright—too bright. She closed her eyes and a vision came into focus. She found herself running from shiny, metal horses that breathed fire. She could feel the heat on her skin, the tears streaming down her cheeks, as she ran for her life—and saw that real animals, propped up with a vacant look in their eyes, watched on. She snapped her eyes open, breathing heavily. Her friends were asleep still, and she was glad they couldn't see her in such a state. Her visions haunted her, as did the memory of the last time she'd rushed to Fairmount with the Elder in the dark of night. He'd died shortly after.

After several days, they stumbled across the banks of the Fluvian River, and not long after that, the cliffs of Fairmount appeared to the north. Gwen saw the straight path along the river curve toward the familiar, imposing rock face. The night she'd arrived with the Elder, she remembered seeing him bow before the True King. She'd thought her troubles were over then. But they were only just beginning. Now they were here to find an army, and face the very king in Gwen's vision who struck Bailey down.

She looked up ahead at Annika, Hal, and Tori. In the moonlight she could make out Bailey's profile, and she hoped to Nature to keep him safe.

Fifteen

THE SUN SET AS they drew closer to the cliffs, and Bailey saw the orange glow of evening light reflecting off the marble façade of the library. His heart leapt. It felt as if he was coming home.

Still, the mood was tense. They didn't know what they'd find as they dismounted their cycles and leaned them against a stone. Annika instructed them on how to cover the bikes with dead, fallen branches before hiking away from the river. Bailey and Gwen walked by the woman's side with Hal and Tori close at their heels.

"What do you think has happened here since we left?" Hal asked. No one was willing to venture a guess, but Bailey couldn't help but think the worst—that Viviana would never give up looking for him or Tremelo.

The pathway up the hill led them to the southwest edge of the school grounds, near the Scavage pitch and the tree house where

Gwen had stayed that winter. He saw her glance toward it, and with her red hair pulled back from her face he could see her far-away expression. She was taking the separation from Phi hard, but Bailey knew there was something else. It wasn't the right time to ask, and he wasn't sure if he should press her again.

From there, the trees thinned, and the school came into view. On the crest of the hill lay the Fairmount Academy, its tall windows catching the warm light of the sun as it set.

"Would you look at that?" Tori said, a bit of awe and fear in her voice. The school gave off the eerie feel of a ghost town.

Silently, they walked up the hill with Taleth, protective and alert, in front of them. The quietness of the grounds disturbed Bailey—he hadn't realized how the usual bustle of everyday school life had seemed so normal before. Now he started at the slightest crack of a twig underneath one of their feet, or the lightest breeze shuffling the branches in the trees behind them.

Tori ran ahead to investigate the Applied Sciences building. The upper floors had been entirely deserted. Tremelo's office had been ransacked, with papers and tinkering parts hastily scattered across his desk and on the floor.

"There's no one," said Tori, scooping up a metal gear from the floor. "Where did they all go?"

"You think they were taken?" Hal asked, adjusting his glasses.

"Let's look in the library," said Bailey, fighting away images of his classmates rounded up and taken away by the Dominae, or worse, killed by uncaring Dominae soldiers. He led his friends toward the clock tower, slowly taking in the emptiness surrounding them. Bailey remembered it had all started here, on the night they found the Loon's book in the library's secret room.

Taleth padded up the marble staircase ahead of them, and Annika walked slowly with a knife in her hand. As they passed the glass bookcase on the second floor hallway, they saw it had been broken—shards of glass everywhere, and books ripped from their shelves. If the Loon's book had been there, it would've been found and put right into Viviana's hands. Bailey shared a look with Tori, who nodded stoically and held her bag to her chest tightly. Thank Nature for her quick thinking.

Just then, they heard a clatter from the other side of the atrium. A piece of wood that had been leaning against the walls of a study room had come tumbling down to the floor. Annika spun around, ready to release her knife on the person who'd snuck up on them, but Hal grabbed her arm and pulled it down. "No!" he yelled. Standing across from the study room was Taylor. He looked as though he was seeing the books behind them leap off the shelves and perform a ballet.

"I was on clock tower duty and had to see for myself," Taylor said, his eyes wide.

"That's my brother," Hal told Annika.

Sensing it was safe, Taylor ran toward them.

"Hal! I was so worried about you," Taylor said, squeezing Hal to his chest and knocking his glasses askew. Bailey met Hal's eyes, which were wide with shock. "I thought you were dead! First, you just disappear for weeks, and then that terrible Fair. . . . I saw Bailey, up on the stage, with Viviana herself—what was going on there, Walker?—but then everything was happening at once, and I couldn't see if you were there too. Shonfield managed to get most of us out and onto a rigi back to school, but I had no idea where you were! Mom and Dad are worried sick. . . ." He still hadn't let go of Hal, who patted Taylor's back.

"Well, I'm okay," Hal said, his voice muffled by the sleeve of Taylor's coat. "But what happened to you?"

"Me?" said Taylor. "I got a nasty bump on the head when the looters came. I fought them off!"

"*You* fought them?" asked Tori drily.

"Well, I *helped*," Taylor said sheepishly, then caught himself. "And what's that supposed to mean? You think I couldn't fight off some Dominae scum?"

Tori only shrugged, and Bailey caught himself snorting.

"What was that, Walker?" said Taylor, his tone suddenly much more familiar to Bailey. "I pulled two students out of the clutches of the Dominae and got knocked on the head! What have you done, eh? You and your creepy lizard kin. Where is that stinking thing, anyway?"

Bailey felt almost relieved to see Taylor back in fighting form. If he'd continued being nice, the next moment wouldn't have been half as satisfying.

"Bert the iguana does not stink," Bailey said defensively. He was a good little guy, and he was with the Velyn back in the tunnels now, with good people who'd care for him. "I'm with my real kin now." He stood back to reveal the archway where Taleth stood. She shook her head, causing her whiskers to tremble.

"Um . . . uh . . ." Taylor stumbled backward, his mouth opening and closing like a stunned fish. His tortoiseshell cat hissed and jumped away.

"Nature's own eyes," someone said. Ms. Shonfield, her face and

ANIMAS

hands streaked with ash, stood at the entrance to the atrium. "Mr.
Walker, Mr. Quindley, Miss Colubride! And . . . and . . ." She looked
between Taleth and Annika, shaking her head. "Where did your
new friends come from? How have you—"

"I just found them, Ms. Shonfield," said Taylor.

"What's happened here?" Bailey asked. "Who did this to the
school?"

"Why don't you all come with me, and I'll explain on the way,"
Shonfield said. "It'll be dark soon, and unsafe to be poking around
in here. We've had a great many thieves come prowling around
from Stillfall, and even farther, since the school burned. Come
along."

Bailey introduced Annika to Shonfield.

"You're in charge?" Annika asked, the knife still in her hand.

"I most certainly am," Shonfield said firmly. "Fairmount is my
home."

Annika seemed impressed, and tucked the knife back in her
boot before shaking the woman's hand. They fell into step, walking
silently like two old friends, and it warmed Bailey's heart to connect
people who were for the goodness of the bond.

Shonfield kept looking over at Taleth with something between
fear and tearful joy in her eyes. The girls walked just behind them,
with Taylor in the rear, his arm around Hal's shoulders.

"Where have you been, little brother?" Bailey heard Taylor ask.
"You aren't hurt, are you?"

"When everything went haywire at the Fair, I managed to
round up most of our students and load them onto the last rigimotive leaving the city," said Shonfield. "I'd had a feeling all morning
that something unpleasant was in store. That assistant of mine—"

"Jerri," Bailey said.

"Yes, Jerri—he skulked away just after Viviana came round with the judges of the Science Competition, and . . . well, I'm naturally curious, and entitled to know what my employees are up to, I think, when they're meant to be chaperoning a school event. . . . I followed him, and saw him march right up to Viviana's private tents. Just a nod to the guard, as if they were old friends. My gut told me to get the students out, and I did the best I could on my own. By the time we were all lined up and ready to leave, the students' animals had begun acting very strangely—"

"What happened here at Fairmount afterward?" Bailey asked.

Shonfield shook her head.

"Things were quiet for a time, but followers of the Dominae arrived that evening. By the following morning we were overtaken by soldiers and folks who fancied themselves part of Viviana's army. They ransacked the school, looking for something or someone— and we were entirely occupied for several nights. Then, when at last they gave up finding what they wanted, they left the same way they came."

She paused, and gestured around them. Bailey and the others slowed their steps, and Taylor walked forward to stand beside her.

"The Dominae seem to have a knack for destruction," Annika said, her jaw tight.

"They've certainly done worse than this," Shonfield responded. "In the town, rumors are they've turned neighbors against one another and encouraged reporting of family and friends if they're Melore loyalists."

"So they were looking for us—or for Tremelo," said Tori, nodding. "They thought we'd come back to the school."

"A storied institution, once the pride of the kingdom, looted from the inside out," Shonfield said. "Not everyone is accounted for. Most of the students ran away, back to their homes, I hope. Most teachers too. Finch is traveling to neighboring towns to appeal for help and temporary shelter for the remaining students, and in the meantime we've been here."

She pointed down the hill to the Scavage pitch. From here, Bailey could see what had been hidden from the bottom of the hill earlier: a makeshift shelter built onto the existing locker rooms of the Scavage field, with a cheery glow emanating from within.

"It's perfectly positioned for an easy retreat in case more Dominae come again. We've got supplies from the dining hall down there, and while Mrs. Copse isn't the most ingenious cook, there's hot food to be had," Ms. Shonfield said. "We take turns on clock tower duty, which is where Taylor was when he found you." She led them down the hill and onto the pitch. Upon reaching the haphazardly nailed door on the temporary build-out, Shonfield knocked twice and called out:

"I sing a song of dear Fairmount..."

"Where the crow flies o'er the squirrel!" a voice sang back. The door opened, and Bailey saw at least two dozen faces of his fellow students peering at him and his friends.

"You'll never guess who we've found up in the library," Ms. Shonfield said, her voice taking an almost unnaturally cheerful tone. "Mr. Walker, Miss Colubride, Mr. Quindley, and..." She stopped at Gwen, and pursed her lips as though embarrassed to have forgotten a name.

"Oh, you don't know me," said Gwen kindly. "Miss Teller. Gwen."

"I didn't know you had a last name" said Hal.

"*Everyone* has a last name," said Tori. Then, to Gwen, "It's nice."

The room was silent for a moment, long enough for Bailey to wonder if, after all, he and his friends weren't welcome there. But then the shock on his classmates' faces disappeared, and he heard several shouts at once as they all clambered up from their benches to greet him.

"Where have you *been*?"

"The school was on lockdown for weeks!"

"Where's your lizard?"

"Where are you from, Red?"

"Did you fight the Dominae?"

"How did you get away?"

"What about Tremelo?"

"I heard he's a spy! Is it true?"

Annika sat with Shonfield and a few teachers who had stayed. Bailey was swept onto a seat and handed a bowl of warm oat porridge with a slap of King's Finger butter on top. As the porridge warmed his insides, he was able to make out individual faces and voices out of the melee—Arabella, captain of his Scavage squad, was there, as well as his teammates Alice, Terrence, and more. Two of Taylor's Year Three friends were helping pass bowls of food. Even Hal and Tori sat in the thick of it, as if they'd been part of the team the whole time. He missed Phi now more than ever.

Gwen couldn't seem to get comfortable, despite plenty of friendly faces—and when she got up to wander to the adults' table, Bailey asked her to stay, and made room at the table next to him.

"Is it true that you're the one the Dominae have been looking for?" asked Arabella, who sat at a bench opposite Bailey.

Bailey looked at Gwen, then back at Arabella, unsure how much to say.

"We didn't have to lie when they were here—none of us knew where you were," Arabella continued.

"But we would have!" squeaked Terrence. "They're terrible."

"Yes, we thought for sure they'd kill you!" said Alice. "But we don't know why!"

"I'll show you why," said Bailey, standing. He walked to the door and looked out. Still sitting in the snow was Taleth. He held out his hand, against which she nuzzled her forehead.

"This is why they want to kill me," Bailey said. "This is my kin. My *real* kin, Taleth."

He stood aside to allow Taleth to enter. The students gasped. More than one bowl of porridge clattered onto the floor. Taleth sat down on the earthen floor of the shelter and licked her front paw, as though too humble to notice that she was being admired by an entire roomful of people.

"They'd kill me because of some prophecy about the last White Tiger Animas in the kingdom," Bailey said. "That's what the Dominae are really like. They don't care about us, or our school, or our families. But we're going to fight them."

Bailey lay awake, thinking it strange to be so close to his dorm but unable to sleep there. Instead, he was sprawled across the hard floor with his friends at his side, wondering how he'd raise an army. Hal was sound asleep, snoring, and Tori looked at peace in the moonlight. But he saw a flash of red—Gwen shuffling in her spot.

"Are you awake?" he whispered, sitting up.

Gwen turned to him and sat up. She nodded, pushing her short curls out of her face. "You okay?" she asked.

"I'm worried," Bailey said. "I'm glad to be back, and that most everyone is okay . . . but what about the symbol of peace? And the army?"

"I don't know," she admitted, rubbing her eyes. "I think about it too, though."

"But you're a Seer, you could . . ."

"I could what?" asked Gwen. "Rewrite it? Re-envision all the prophecies the Loon had?"

He could hear the defensiveness in her voice and tried to tread carefully. "No, I didn't mean it like that. I just meant maybe there was something we were missing?"

"Maybe," said Gwen, flinging her blanket up suddenly. "Obviously, I'm not a very good Seer. I'm sorry I got it all wrong and led us all the way to the Dust Plains and back."

"That's not what I meant! I'm not blaming you or anyone!" Bailey said in a hoarse whisper. "I'm just frustrated. It's been one riddle after the other. Sometimes I just want to know the answer is even there—like when they give you the practice answers in the back of the textbook. I don't check it every time but just for some reassurance, you know?"

"I think so." Gwen hugged her knees to her chest. "Not the textbook part, really—but I know what you mean. I'm worried too. Like, the more time that passes the more uncertain I am about the passage in the book. What if it's just some goose chase?"

"But you have visions, don't you? Can't you tap into that again and tell us what our next move should be?"

"You think my visions can save us?" Gwen said loudly. Tori stirred. "As far as what will happen next, maybe I can see it and maybe I can't. But some visions of the future are..." Gwen trailed off.

"They're what?" Bailey asked. Tori was sitting up now, and she nudged Hal awake. He felt like he was on the verge of cracking Gwen open, seeing what had been upsetting her all these weeks.

It looked as though Gwen was ready to speak, but the clock tower rang out and Bailey's blood went cold. They'd been told earlier that the bell had been disabled and only went off if the person on watch duty saw something in the distance.

"Is it the Dominae?" someone asked.

Suddenly, students were getting up in a frenzy, and teachers did their best to direct everyone in the dark as they fled into the woods.

"Hang on a minute," Hal said, tilting his head as if he were trying to hear what his bats heard. Other students streamed past them. "There's a mustelid coming."

"A what?" Gwen asked. Bailey didn't know, either.

"A short-legged mammal," Tori clarified.

"I think... it's a badger!" Hal said, weaving his way against the current of the crowd.

"Mr. Quindley!" Shonfield called out. But Hal moved faster and with more agility than Bailey had ever seen him, running across the benches between locker rows before anyone could stop him. Bailey and his friends followed not too far behind as he busted through the front doors and onto the Scavage pitch. Sure enough, there was a badger emerging from the nearby woods, laboring across the field. Hal ran to it and knelt down just as the animal collapsed in his arms. It was one of Uncle Roger's kin.

Roger, Digby, and the familiar faces of the RATS followed. Bailey and his friend cheered, and tore across the field to meet them. But he nearly stopped in his tracks when he saw a hare hop up the crest of the hill, sniffing the air as it regarded him.

Longfoot. His dad's life-bonded kin.

And behind him, there were his mom and dad—just as he'd left them in the Lowlands. His dad's hair was a familiar mess of curls.

His mom dropped everything she was carrying and ran toward him. "Bailey!" she called, just like she used to when she would coax him outside to enjoy the heavy autumn rains. His own feet carried him forward quickly, and before he knew up from down he was in his mom's arms. She lifted him off the ground a few inches. Emily wasn't tall, but she was strong. His dad was a split second behind and wrapped the two of them in an even bigger hug.

"We were so worried!" Herman said. "Where have you been?"

Bailey felt his mom's tears against his face. "After Viviana Melore's Progress Fair, we—"

But his mom gasped before he could finish, and tumbled out the story of how his father had been scouring the nearby towns for any Fairmount students and teachers who might know Bailey. When the Dominae started to take over the Lowlands, a handful of locals found the tunnels and led all the townspeople there.

"And by some miracle of Nature, we met the RATS and now we're here!" his mom cried, squeezing him even tighter.

Bailey knew intuitively that Taleth was stalking toward him.

He pulled back from his mom and lowered himself onto the ground to see his kin coming down the field, her ears back and her tail lowered. Everyone else on the field paused to watch her, and the closer she got, the harder his parents clutched him. But even they sensed something was happening.

Ten feet away, she stopped and lay down on her stomach—her paws extended in front of her. Bailey turned back to his parents and motioned his head toward Taleth. "Come on," he said gently. He grabbed his mom's hand and she grabbed his dad's, and together, all three of them walked toward Taleth. She swung her tail back and forth softly. When they approached, he pressed his palm to her forehead, and felt how badly she wanted to put his parents at ease. He shared the sentiment.

"Mom, Dad," Bailey said. "I had my Awakening...."

His mom burst into tears and pulled him into another hug.

"How about that," his father kept repeating, putting his hand out for Taleth to nudge.

"You're the one they're talking about!" his mom said. "Tell us everything."

And so right there on the field, he told his parents everything. "And you've met Tremelo?" he asked. "My professor?"

They shared a look of concern.

"About Mr. Tremelo," Digby said from behind them. His face was crestfallen as he twisted his cap in his hands. "Not sure any other way to say this, except that he's gone."

Sixteen

PHI DREAMED MORE IN Defiance than she ever had before in her life.

She'd never slept well growing up, and now she tended not to remember dreams, except as slippery, quick images that darted through her waking mind just once, only to disappear as soon as she opened her eyes. But in Defiance, under the care of the Tully, she lost herself each night so deeply that when she woke, she was almost sad to see herself returned to reality.

She dreamed, each night, of flying.

"You're healing well," said the Tully one morning, just as Phi was opening her eyes. "Soon we'll be able to deliver you to your friends."

"WAKE UP!" Lukas called from the foot of the bed, as he had every morning. Phi groaned, not wanting the dream to shake off just yet. She'd been flying alongside Carin, over a vast forest. Ahead, the river twisted and turned like a curled blue ribbon.

"Let her be, just a bit longer, little lizard," said the Tully to her son. "She's dreaming of wings."

On her perch by Phi's bed, Carin squawked, as if in agreement. Phi stared at the Tully. How had she known?

"You're among like folk here," said the Tully in response to Phi's silence. "There's not a woman in Defiance who hasn't once wished she were something besides herself."

"How can you tell that about me?" asked Phi. She'd told no one about her secret: her desperation to become a bird. At times, she thought that Bailey had guessed, and Gwen as well. Tori, she knew, had read her journal. But they were her friends. In front of the Tully and Lukas, near strangers, she felt exposed.

"How could I not?" said the Tully. "Little thing like you, so uncomfortable in your own skin."

Phi clenched the blankets in her hands. The Tully shuffled from one end of the tent to the other, carrying a pitcher of fresh water.

Lukas tilted his head at her. "But you can help, can't you, Mam?"

"Help?" Phi asked. "Help how?"

"Make you into your kin!" Lukas said.

"I cannot," said the Tully as she gave her son the side-eye. "The boy misunderstands."

"I didn't misunderstand anything!" Lukas argued. "There was the one time when you turned that woman in—"

"*Enough*, Lukas," the Tully said firmly. Phi had never heard the woman call him by his given name. "Why don't we finish up our morning chores and let her rest?"

"I am rested. I've *been* resting," said Phi. "Please tell me."

The Tully pinched her wrinkled lips together and breathed in through her nose. After what seemed to Phi to be a very long, tense moment, the Tully shook her head and opened the flap of the tent. She motioned her head for Lukas to follow. He stole a quick glance at Phi and hopped off the bed.

"See you later. . . ." he said. Phi only nodded, her thoughts filled with what it could all mean.

The women of Defiance had insisted Phi rest, and rest, and then rest some more. She tried to help with collecting firewood or foraging for vegetables, but she'd been sent back to bed several times. In truth, she had only wanted to keep her hands busy to quiet her mind. She didn't dare ask about the woman Lukas spoke of, the one whom the Tully helped—but she thought about her constantly.

By sunset she'd regained her strength, and found Lukas inspecting rocks on the outer skirts of the camp. When she arrived, he'd proudly showed her rocks of brilliant colors that he took with him from place to place, since it was true that Defiance was a town that moved often. Phi inspected the rocks, judging them for herself to be truly beautiful. But there was an ulterior motive even she couldn't deny.

"What you said earlier," Phi started. "What did you mean? About your mam helping a woman?"

He turned back to his rocks, his back stiffening. "Mam said not to say."

Phi lowered herself to sit on the soil, suddenly hit with a dizzy spell. She knew she wouldn't press it. She'd worked herself up with myth and magic, and whatever she'd imagined was probably impossible. But even if Lukas wasn't supposed to talk, he was eager to.

He spun around with a striped rock of deep red and white in his little hand. "I found this one the day the woman came," he said in nearly a whisper. Phi leaned forward as he continued. "We were near the edge of the kingdom, near the Underlands. She was tired, I remember that—but lots of people who join us are tired."

Phi nodded.

"But she was special, I guess. She wanted to change into her kin. I was there! Mam said she could help her, and called it 'a forsaking,'" he said. "But she told the woman that she'd have to say good-bye to what was dearest to her."

Phi considered this—she thought she knew what it meant. She, the Phi that lived in this body, had a family and friends. Would she be able to communicate with them, if she became an animal? Or would she forget them? But something kept pulling her on—the wish she'd felt inside of her, for her entire life.

"And could your mam help this woman?" she asked.

Lukas nodded, his floppy hair falling in front of his eyes. "I helped her."

Phi pulled her knees to her chest and went very still. "What happened?"

"We collected herbs all morning, and Mam pulled out her giant book and followed a recipe. I wasn't there for that part. I only know the next day the woman was gone, but there were huge paw tracks from her tent...."

Phi felt as though even a breath could make what she'd just heard untrue. "Do you remember the herbs?" she asked.

Lukas looked away; she couldn't see his face. "You want to try it for yourself," he said.

"If I don't try it, I'll always wonder . . ." Phi said, trailing off. "I've lived my whole life thinking I don't belong—that if I never get to experience what my kin feels, I'll die. Of longing or sadness."

She stopped herself, feeling silly for pouring her heart out like that in front of a child.

"I can't help—I can't get in trouble with Mam," he said.

"I'd never want that," Phi said, and she meant it.

Lukas started back up toward the tents, looking out at the darkness of the desert. He paused, and without turning he called back to her: "But I can tell you Mam keeps the book at the foot of her sleeping mat. . . ."

Seventeen

"HE WAS TAKEN!" BAILEY yelled, conscious of how everyone backed away—as if he were a wild animal.

"The Velyn heard him mouth off before he left," Roger argued. "'Why bother trying to save the kingdom?' he'd said. Then he disappeared in the dead of night."

"The boy could still be right," Merrit said, a sheepdog sniffing in circles by his feet. "We don't know what the Velyn saw or heard."

"Right!" Bailey said. "Surely he didn't mean it. He was just blowing off steam, probably. Digby! Tell them!"

He shrugged nervously, wiping the sweat from his brow despite how cool the night air was. "Bailey, it's hard to explain. I knew Tremelo as a child and sometimes he'd get an itch and need to scratch it. He hadn't had a lot of supervision growing up. He was free to wander, so perhaps..."

Bailey paced back and forth. "He wouldn't wander! Not at a

time like this! We need to go and find him!" He wanted to burn off the anger, to run deep into the woods and find him right this second.

Taleth, for her part, had left to run through the woods. Best for everyone, he figured. They were agitated, but it didn't mean that anyone needed to get hurt. She'd come back when she was ready and when Bailey was calmer. If he was ever calmer.

"I agree with Bailey," Tori said. "No way he'd cut and run, not after what we saw at the Progress Fair."

"And he was in the middle of tinkering with something to counteract the Dominae effects. Even if he wanted to leave this sorry lot, he wouldn't leave a half-finished project!" Hal said, nodding furiously at his own point.

That sparked a big argument, with everyone talking over everyone else. Bailey suggested a search party, but the adults refused to consider letting him actually lead said search party. In the flurry of voices, Bailey noticed one was conspicuously absent. Gwen twisted a strand of red hair, looking at the ground with a thoughtful frown on her face.

"What do you think, Gwen?" he asked. It was one of those rare moments that there'd been a lull in the arguing, and now all eyes were on her.

She dropped her hand away from her hair and straightened up. "It's—it's hard to tell," she stuttered. "He was under a lot of pressure. What if he did just leave?"

"But what if he didn't!" Bailey said. "He could need our help! Because I know we need his if we want to actually defeat Viviana."

He couldn't believe that Gwen of all people could doubt Tremelo, after everything the Elder sacrificed for him.

A compromise was finally reached: they would spend the evening searching the school grounds for anything prophecy related—and in the morning they'd send out a small search party, including Bailey, to backtrack to the tunnels and see if Tremelo had left anything that might help them locate him.

The Scavage team quickly took to organizing itself as they searched high and low through the school, well past dinnertime to the chagrin of Mrs. Copse. They were looking for the symbol of peace the Loon's book spoke of, but they had to take precautions in case the looters came back. The Sneaks and Slammers fanned out around the group, each player wary to spot any trouble ahead. The Squats, with Bailey and Taleth alongside them, formed a perimeter around the younger students, the way they would protect their team's flag during a game. Shonfield had insisted she come along, and marched with Annika and the students, requesting head counts each hour of the search. The RATS and Bailey's parents stayed with the remainder of the students back in the locker rooms, eager to rest.

"I'd never expected to think of myself as a military officer," Shonfield mused. "But I suppose it's not very different from being an administrator, is it?"

As for Bailey, the familiar parts of Fairmount he'd known— the square, the clock tower from where he'd jumped just months before, the dormitories—all looted. If he wasn't already antsy about Tremelo's disappearance, this wasn't helping brighten his mood. He still couldn't understand why anyone would believe he willingly abandoned them. That wasn't the king Bailey knew.

Shonfield transitioned between military leader and principal. As she showed Annika the keystones of the school, she did so with pride, and Bailey could see that Annika listened with genuine interest.

"Really?" Annika asked. "Two hundred years old!"

"At least!" Shonfield said proudly of the gray stone that made up the fireplace of the library. "We're standing in the oldest part of the school, the first thing built, really. For hundreds of years, students, teachers, and visitors alike have been surrounded by books and stones in this very spot. Funny how schools are so much like fortresses, don't you think? And the army within its walls is the very knowledge that is learned, discussed, circulated—"

"Mrs. Shonfield!" Tori said, looking up at the principal. "You're a genius!"

Their administrator's eyes widened in pleasant surprise; it was uncommon for Tori to be so complimentary. "Why, thank you, Ms. Colubride, but really I'm sure I read that sentiment somewhere—"

But Tori was shaking her head excitedly, her snakes slithering back toward her through the crowd of students. "Did you all hear that?" she asked Bailey, Gwen, and Hal. "What if the 'wise army' from the Loon's book isn't a *fighting* army? What if it's an army of knowledge—an army of books?"

"You're onto something!" Gwen exclaimed.

"There are hundreds of books here!" Hal said.

"But what's the best thing to read in preparation for battle?"

"A fighting manual?" Hal asked.

Tori nudged him in the ribs. "No. The politics and history section!"

"'History repeats itself. . . .'" Gwen said, quoting a long-known phrase.

Bailey's chest expanded like a balloon; did they have the answer needed to finally decipher the Loon's words?

"What are we waiting for?" he asked, and led the charge with Taleth up to the history section on the second floor, nearly tripping on books scattered across the stairs. They each pulled off armfuls of books at a time, as Shonfield implored someone to tell her what in Nature was going on. But the friends remained focused, and soon the rest of the students were flipping through pages and quoting any passages of the Melorian reign that might seem relevant.

As more and more books disappeared off the shelves and into the laps of eager readers, Bailey realized there was a shape carved into the stone wall—partially obscured by the books that remained. He put his own book down, opened to a section on agricultural reform and the debate to use animals to help plow fields.

"Where are you going?" Hal asked, but Bailey ignored him, now fixated on the shape. He removed books off the shelf, two or three at a time, until the shape started to become bigger. It expanded on the stone wall, and Hal began to help, until the shelves were empty and all that was left was a large crest of Melore—a slim, sharp pentagon—and at the very center, a sword affixed.

"Anting Nature's eyes!" Tori said.

"Language," Shonfield murmured, but everyone knew she didn't care. The entire library was in a stunned silence, and Bailey felt frozen in his steps—finally facing the thing he'd sought this entire time. The prophecy that they'd pursued, that had cost them the company of both Tremelo and Phi.

"Go on!" Hal said.

Bailey reached for it and could feel the vibration strengthen as his hand came closer yet. When he grabbed the hilt, a jolt of power coursed through his body, the bond strengthened so that he felt Taleth's presence like never before. She purred behind them. Bailey knew, intuitively, that it was made of the same metal as Viviana's machine—but it was stronger, more powerful. And more important, if its bearer wanted to do good, then so would the metal.

The clock tower rang out—a sure sign of alarm, and for a moment it caused everyone to pause. From outside, Terrence, a Year Two Sneak, entered with the news.

"There's some kind of fight happening in the woods just outside the school," he said. "Alice saw a volley of arrows shot into the air, and the other side is launching rocks and cannonballs into the trees!"

"Viviana's come back!" Gwen exclaimed.

"Did you see any of the fighters?" Bailey asked Terrence. "Can you describe them?"

Terrence shook his head. "We'll have to get closer," he said.

"You'll do no such thing!" said Shonfield. All the students held their breath. "Not all at once, at least," she continued. "We'll need reconnaissance. Who here has avian kin?"

Bailey glanced at Gwen. She didn't meet his eyes. Whether she was thinking of Phi, whose bond with Carin could have helped them, or her own severed bond, Bailey couldn't tell. He felt a tug at his heart, even though he still wanted to be mad at her for doubting Tremelo.

Hal raised his hand.

"I'm not avian, but my kin can fly," he said.

A few minutes later, Bailey stood with the sword in his hand next to Hal, Taylor, and Annika on a rocky ledge overlooking the woods beyond the school. Taleth, Tori, Gwen, Shonfield, and the rest of the students stood or crouched behind them on the rocks. From the trees opposite them, they heard crashes and shouts. Hal took a deep breath.

"Okay," he said quietly, shutting his eyes.

A sound like wind through dead leaves grew in volume. Bailey turned to look behind them, and saw a sizeable cloud of bats rising up from the branches of the forest and careening toward him and Hal. Hal clenched his eyes tightly, and the bats flew just over the heads of all those watching, spreading out over the valley. Once they reached the other side, they disappeared into the trees.

Hal did not speak for a moment, and then he opened his eyes wide.

"It's Defiance!" he said.

And as if on cue, the top of a sail poked up from behind a cluster of rocks. Bailey and Hal, with Gwen, Tori, and Annika right behind them, scrambled down into the trench below them to get a closer look. On the other side of the rocky valley was "docked" one of the land ships of Defiance.

"How did it get *here*?" Hal asked.

As if the ship itself were answering him, four small hatches opened on the ship's bottom with a squeak, and out of each one emerged a mechanical leg. The legs planted themselves and lifted the ship from the rocks.

"Right," Hal said. "How could I have forgotten the walking ship?"

A figure appeared on the deck, carrying a heavy-looking round object.

"It's the Tully!" said Bailey. He stood up tall and waved his arms.

"Tully!" Annika yelled out. "Stop this madness!"

The Tully ducked as a volley of arrows struck the side of the ship, from the direction of the forest.

"Fire!" yelled a voice, and the round object that the Tully had just been carrying soared out of a cannon on the side of the ship. It crashed into the trees, where Bailey heard the splintering of a struck tree falling.

"Oh Nature's ears," said Tori. "Digby and the RATS have fired on them!"

"Stop!" shouted Gwen, joining Bailey as she waved alongside him.

"She can't hear you over all that noise," said Annika. "I'll have to get closer and tell them."

"Then Hal and I will come with you!" Tori said, as the three began to climb down toward the Tully.

"We'll go find Digby?" Bailey asked Gwen. She nodded and they were off. "Stay there where it's safe!" Bailey implored Shonfield and the other students. He and Gwen ran to the embankment of rocks that would lead to the other side of the trench. Taleth leapt down to join them. The sounds of whooshing arrows and the crashing of the Tully's cannon echoed as they climbed up and into the cover of the trees. He wished Tremelo was here to talk some sense into everyone.

Even through the noise, Bailey and Gwen had no trouble finding their bearings in the woods, as Digby Barnes's loud voice echoed through the trees. "Come out, you snail-slime, and fight us in the open!"

Bailey and Gwen followed the sound of his bellowing to a sun-spattered grove. Just north, through a thin line of trees, an open hillside offered a view of the higher peaks beyond. In the grove just beyond the pitch, the RATS and the Velyn crouched in fighting positions, weapons aimed at the trees directly south of them.

"And . . . fire!" shouted Digby to a flank of archers.

"Wait!" shouted Gwen. "Digby, stop!"

The arrows soared over Gwen's and Bailey's heads and struck the trunks of the trees behind them.

"At least we know the Tully and her fighters aren't even *in* the trees," Gwen muttered.

Bailey kept his head down and ran from one boulder to another with the sword clutched tightly in his hand. He was inching closer to the Allies' firing line. Gwen and Taleth kept close behind him, with Gwen occasionally popping up between volleys to yell out Digby's name. Finally, just as the Velyn were about to release their arrows, Digby saw them.

"What in Nature?" he shouted. "Stop. Cease fire, everyone! It's the kids!"

Gwen and Bailey ran to him.

"You have to stop fighting," Bailey gasped, out of breath.

"Not a chance—they attacked first! These . . . these . . . hooligans with their wooden cannonballs and their sneaky ways! Blast them! They haven't shown so much as a whisker or claw—nasty hard creatures to see!"

Digby ducked as a whooshing cannonball soared over their heads and smashed, sending splinters of wood everywhere, into the trunk of the tree behind them.

"You'll have to do better than that!" Digby yelled.

"No, you don't understand," said Gwen. "We know them—they're friends!"

"Some friends," said Digby. "You show me a 'friend' that shoots without bein' introduced proper, and I'll show you a muskrat's musk."

"Bailey! Gwen!" Tori's voice floated over the Allies' ranks from the edge of the grove.

"Over here!" shouted Bailey.

Annika appeared out of the shadows, leading the Tully and Lukas. Tori and Hal were just a step behind. Annika frowned, her strong chin jutted forward, as though she was annoyed at everyone for playing war.

"Sorry about that last whizz-bang," said the Tully, a hand cupped around her wrinkled mouth. "It was already loaded when these three came to fetch us!"

"Digby Barnes, this is my companion, the Tully," said Annika as the other party approached.

"You're both here to fight for the True King—not one another!" Gwen added.

A long moment of agonized silence settled between the two groups, as Digby wiped his hands on his knees.

"Please," the Tully said, her deep voice low and magical. "Accept our apologies. We were too hasty with the cannons."

"Well, I . . ." said Digby. He'd pulled back a makeshift helmet made of a metal trash receptacle. "No worries at all . . . no harm done. Held our own, didn't we? Yes. Lovely, lovely." Like everyone, he'd humbled himself before the Tully, who had her way with words and people.

"Where is Phi?" Bailey asked. Gwen nodded, her grin wide as she stood on the tips of her toes to get a better view of the landscape.

"She left," Lukas said. He buried his face into the Tully's side.

"Left?" Gwen asked.

Bailey's insides felt like they'd frozen over. "Left where?" he asked.

Lukas shook his head as if he was ashamed.

"What's done is done, little lizard," the Tully said gently. "Tell them where she is, *what* she is...."

Lukas pointed up. "She's a bird in the sky now."

Eighteen

PHI SOARED ABOVE THE Dark Woods. The wind caught under her wings, and she felt the wisps slip through the ends of her individual feathers, creating a strange mix of buoyancy and instability that she had to quickly learn to control. And her wings, themselves—they were as beautiful as they were sturdy. She'd always admired Carin's coloring, the fine places where tan stopped and dark, rich brown began. But never had she appreciated their perfect design, all the better to cut through the air, until now.

How had she gotten here? There was a vague memory of Phi's human mind—gathering and crushing herbs in a stone bowl, breathing in the spices as she chanted in the darkness. It had hit the back of her throat and her nostrils like sparks from a camp-fire, where it seemed to stick and continue burning. She couldn't breathe. Her hands had reached out, grasping for water, for air, for kindness.

And then she'd seen those same hands split and flatten. Her fingers became feathers, and suddenly the dark horizon rose up in front of her vision as her feet hardened and shrank. She scrambled on a nearby tree with thick, sharp talons that cut haphazardly into the bark. They'd ached, these new feet, as though the old ones had been literally ripped away. She tried to speak then, but all she heard was a loud shriek that filled her own ears. Her mouth was so long, so hard and curved, and the sound that came out from it had been as sharp as a rigimotive's whistle.

The last thing she remembered was the last thing her human eyes had read: *The risk is high. And if the human does not return to her original form after due time, she is bound to the shape of her kin forever.* And yet even now, she could grasp that it wasn't a risk. Forever in this form wouldn't be long enough.

Now, Carin joined her—and she was filled with a sense of belonging and rightness. Together they flew in barrel rolls, circling each other in loops. They shot through dense thickets of trees, ducking over and under branches with not even a scratch. Phi's bird-eyes saw the forest in wide spans, swiveling to find the best berries, the softest stoats, which she and Carin shared like family.

Just then, she spotted two other birds in the distance. They approached, gliding menacingly on large wings. Before too long it became clear they were cutting a path toward Phi and Carin. Carin dipped and swooped around, screeching for Phi to follow her back the way they came. Phi's breath caught in her throat as she tried to execute the same maneuver, but she still wasn't used to her wings. The two birds separated as if to circle around them, their movements efficient but unnatural. Predators. Phi's heart, already beating so much faster than it ever had in her old life, began to vibrate.

One of the strange birds pursued her. No matter what current she rode or how hard she flapped her wings, it gained on her. Where was Carin? She was no longer certain of where she was, and disoriented, she felt it before she understood—a cold beak clamping down on her throat like a vise. She started to screech as blood dripped and matted in the feathers of her chest. The pain! She lifted her talons, scratching at the bird in vain—and she scratched not feathers and flesh but metal. Phi looked at the attacking bird for the first time and saw red, gleaming eyes.

All the knowledge of her human mind rushed back to her, and she had one, overwhelming thought: *Viviana is here.*

Nineteen

OFF THE BATTLEFIELD AND back on the campus, one of the RATS in Digby's charge returned, reporting a black dust at the edge of the forest.

"The site was covered in what looked like ash, with a pair of what looked like hoofprints running straight through," the woman said, showing the black soot on her fingertips. A tawny deer with big eyes waited in the distance, too coy to come any closer. "But not in random, natural patterns. No, these prints here were in a perfect *line*. Like they were machines ..."

Gwen gasped. "Mechanical horses?" she asked. She seemed shaken by the possibility; they all were.

"We'll have to investigate, I suppose," Digby said, kneading his red cap in his hands. He didn't seem to like making decisions all that much.

"But what about Tremelo?" Bailey insisted. "We'd agreed to investigate the school grounds and then lead a search to find him! And now that there's more of us," he said, gesturing to the women of Defiance with his sword-bearing hand, "then all the more reason to go now."

"You guys remember Tremelo, right?" Tori said to the group. "He's only our *king.*"

Digby looked to Merrit and Roger helplessly. But it was Shonfield who stepped in.

"Why don't we send a group out with two goals: to investigate the ash-covered site and search for Tremelo?"

Bailey and his friends couldn't argue with that, and they came along despite initial resistance; it was Tori who threatened that they'd follow just the same if they weren't "allowed" to come along.

Now in the forest, they'd fanned out to find the black soot and tracks. Hal and Bailey stayed close behind Digby and Annika. But when a pair of red eyes glinted in the dense brambles, Bailey called out. Digby and Annika ran toward it, their weapons at the ready. Bailey's heart was doing jumping jacks.

Annika gave Digby a nod, and the man pulled back the branches in one swoop while Annika moved in and yelled, "Surrender!"

In response Bailey heard a man's moan, saw Annika stumble back—less in fear than in surprise. He and Hal ran to her side to see what she saw.

It was a man. He looked battered and thin, on the verge of collapse. He wore an eye patch, but his remaining eye had a look of desperation.

"I surrender," he said in a near whisper. The man was slumped over the back of a metal horse with red eyes. It stared at them coolly but did not move to attack.

"It's a machine," said Hal, "just like those birds!"

"I've seen these," Gwen murmured, quiet enough so that only Bailey could hear. She stepped up to look the horse in its eyes. She got closer than anyone else dared to, but she was scared—Bailey could tell by the way her hand shook.

"My Nature, man," Digby said, somewhat tenderly. "What happened to you?"

The man attempted to dismount the automaton, which was much larger than the Clamoribus, and even taller than Viviana's sharp-clawed tiger had been. But he slipped and would've fallen, had it not been for Digby, who moved to catch him. Once he was secure, Digby eased him to sit on the forest floor.

"My name is Clarke. I'm here for my son..." the man said weakly. "Lyle."

"Lyle?!" Tori piped up. The small group sent out to investigate had now formed behind them.

Annika held out a canteen of water for the man to drink. He could not lift it himself and she helped him, holding it to his mouth while he gulped eagerly and spurted.

Bailey stepped past them and stood next to Gwen, drawn to the horse and terrified at the same time. His mother was Animas Horse, and he'd grown up around the animals—massive, strong, stoic. Reaching up, he lightly touched its nose. It was the same kind of metal as Lyle's orb.

"It's the same as the tiger's heart from the Fair!" Hal said, scooting in between them. He ran a cautious finger along the carved ridge of the horse's nostril. His finger became coated with the same powder that was mixed with the dust outside.

"They're filled with it," he said. "Almost like gunpowder."

Bailey's hands shook. He'd seen firsthand what the Dominae could do. With this kind of power, he didn't want to imagine what Viviana had planned. Now, more than ever, they needed to find Tremelo. He'd know what to do. He'd know how to defeat it.

"They mine, they build, and then they move on," Clarke mumbled. "They're setting up camps."

"Camps?" Gwen asked.

"I helped her. I shouldn't have, I know that now...." Clarke trailed off. He was obviously exhausted. "But I was scared."

Bailey nodded gravely.

"It churned my stomach. They use animals of all kinds to haul and break up the rocks. And I swear, those animals weren't in their own minds. I saw—I saw..."

"What? What was it?" Bailey asked.

"It sounds mad. But I saw a lynx, a little desert cat, moving about as though it was living—but it wasn't."

Bailey and Gwen shared a look; he'd remembered the jackal at the Progress Fair who'd seemingly come back from the dead. He was sure at the time that he'd been mistaken, that the animal had only regained consciousness after being knocked out. But now he wasn't sure. Annika placed a hand on either one of their shoulders to put them at ease.

"Don't ask me how I know; it's too terrible. But its soul wasn't with it. Its eyes were empty. Moved like a puppet, pulling a pallet of rocks. I can't shake the thought of it, no matter how I try. It was Dominance, but something else too...."

Gwen knelt before the battered man and took his hands in her own. He was instantly put at ease by her touch.

"Is there a way to defeat these metal horses?" she asked intensely.

He shifted in his seat, a pained look returning to his face. "No," he said, his voice on the verge of cracking. "They're tainted. Evil. It's as if they feed on your fear, just like Viviana herself." He paused to double over and cough here. When he took his hand away from his mouth, there were drops of blood.

After a stunned silence Digby asked that they let Clarke rest. "Needs to save his breath for his little boy, he does," he added. He picked Clarke up and began to head back to camp.

"Shouldn't half of us stay out and keep looking for Tremelo?" Bailey asked.

"We can't split our forces," Roger said. "And this man clearly needs to get to safety."

Everyone began to walk back toward the school as if a decision had already been made. Bailey fumed, and fell a few steps behind as he gathered his thoughts. He sought Gwen out and wove his way through the small band of people to speak to her.

"Why don't you want to find Tremelo?" he asked her harshly. Her eyes opened wide in surprise.

"I—I do want to find him," she stuttered in response.

"You didn't seem like you did back there at the school," Bailey said. "Tell the adults you want to. They'll listen to you."

"No, they won't!"

"They might! You're from Parliament. You're the Elder's apprentice, and you're older than the rest of us. And anyway it couldn't hurt. I can't do this all by myself!" he said, raising his voice.

Gwen's eyes flashed with anger. "Don't yell at me!" she said, poking her finger into Bailey's chest. "You think just because you have a sword in your hand you can tell me what to do and what to say?"

Bailey stepped back, surprised by her anger. Her Gray accent had come out as well, clipped words and a musical flow to it. But he still wasn't going to back down.

"Admit it: you don't want to find Tremelo," he said. Tori and Hal fell behind the group to see what the commotion was about. "Tell me why."

"I don't want to put you in more danger!" she yelled. "I mean, *us*. I don't want to put us or anyone else in more danger!"

"Fine. I don't care what you do. We'll just go without you! Come on, Hal, Tori." He moved to leave, but Hal grabbed his arm.

"She's right. We can't split off from the group. It's too dangerous," he said. Tori looked down at the ground and brought her hand up to the back of her neck, but she didn't disagree with Hal like Bailey had expected her to.

"You guys too? You're giving up on our king?"

"No!" Tori said, looking up. "But we know we have the sword, the army, and shelter. We should go back and strategize what to do next."

"I already know what to do next!" Bailey said. He pointed with his sword to the east, where the tunnels ran. "I need to go find our king."

He spun around to sprint toward the tunnels before the adults noticed he'd gone missing, but suddenly an overwhelming sensation came over him, and his bond. He nearly fell to the ground.

"Are you all right?" he heard Gwen say, but even her voice was phasing out. Almost immediately he couldn't even hear his blood pounding behind his ears. His skin felt like it was on fire. Taleth nudged him with her flank, and her warmth was a comfort. Her whiskers twitched, alert.

"What's happening?" Bailey whispered to her, as if she could answer in words. Her ears were up, alert. Bailey's vision darted back and forth between what he could see in front of him—his hands, Taleth, the worried faces of his friends—and other trees and rocks, all switching back and forth too quickly, as though he was seeing through several different eyes all at once.

"Bailey, what's going on?" asked Hal. He was aware that all his friends stood around him, concerned looks on their faces. But then Tori gasped and grabbed his arm, pointing beyond the trees toward the hillside just north of them.

At least a dozen white tigers stood there, staring down at him. Bailey dropped to his knees. Taleth nudged him again and then ran to her brethren. Another tiger, this one even larger and with green, wise eyes, paced forward to meet her. They rubbed their foreheads together, and the older tiger nipped at Taleth's ear affectionately.

"Nature's teeth," said Digby.

"Where did they come from?" asked Annika.

"From the other side of the mountains," came her answer, shouted down to them by Tremelo. Eneas Fourclaw stood by his side, and together they strode down the side of the hill, from the same direction as the tigers. Everyone rushed to greet them, shouting their surprise. Everyone, that was, except Bailey.

He could not take his eyes off of the white tigers, still standing in a streak on the hillside. Each pair of eyes on him was like a searchlight, blinding him. His breath came to him in large gasps. The tigers began to move down the hillside toward him, flanking Tremelo on either side. Bailey wiped his hand across his face—he hadn't realized until that moment that he'd been crying.

"They've been waiting for you, boy," said Tremelo, helping him to his feet. "Beyond the limits of Aldermere, they waited until the time was ripe."

"I knew you wouldn't abandon us," said Bailey.

"A ragtag group like you lot," he said looking around. "It's the reason I want to rule."

Bailey shook his head in amazement. He couldn't tear his eyes away from the tigers. "Thank you for bringing them here."

"They came here themselves," he replied. "They came here for you."

Twenty

IT ACHED WHERE THE muscles of Phi's wings met the back of her body. So many times she'd tried to fly away only to get yanked back down. A short leather strap tethered her to a bolt in the ground.

There were lots of other bolts. There had been lots of other falcons, too, but they were gone now. Phi had seen them change, lose their will in order to adopt another's—the man in black. She'd seen her avian kin submit to his Dominance firsthand, and now he was working on her. It was terrifying, like speeding toward the drop of a cliff. Phi didn't know if she could hold out much longer. She could only feel relief that Carin had escaped.

The man in black was already tall for a human, but he towered above Phi's falcon form. He was her kin; she could tell by the immediate pull she felt toward his soul. He wanted to soar just like they all did. Phi felt it. But she could feel, too, how he was a predator—and how this desire to trap and kill was fueled by something other than survival. This man did not want to submit to natural cycles of life and death. All he wanted was to take for the sake of taking.

His arms swung in big arcs, and he paced back and forth. By the beads of sweat she judged his condition. Her human mind remembered so many of those old words: *frustrated*, *tired*, *angry*, *scared*.

These were dark feelings of his will, and Phi resisted. She wouldn't give in to the fear. She thought of how she'd overcome everything terrifying in her life. In a flash, she remembered the contraption she'd made, giant wings that failed her in the thunderstorm—and how it was her friends, always, who came to find her. She knew she was loved, and that was enough to overcome the Dominance. For now.

How long had they been at this? She couldn't think of time passing as she did in her human mind, only notice how the sun had nearly traveled across the entire sky. It was getting dark, and her vision was sharpening. The insects would come out soon, as would the mice, and perhaps she would feed if she could fly as she was meant to.

The human man shifted, and more humans came in through the entrance of the courtyard behind him. A woman was in front, the others streaming behind her as if she were leading an attack formation. Her shoes made sharp, clicking sounds on the pavement as she approached—and stood before Phi as if her violet eyes were searching Phi's soul. She had eyes like a winter sunset. *Purple?* Phi strained to remember. It was another shade like purple, but more delicate. But her mind was fuzzy. Dominance filled up her presence so that Phi could barely feel her own will. She didn't want to fly away. She was powerless.

Then Phi raised her right wing without wanting to, stretching it much too far so that it hurt. She screeched out in pain and felt her voice robbed of her as silence hushed the room. Phi couldn't resist her. It was a woman of nightmares, a woman she remembered from her human form: Viviana.

Then something painful surged through Phi, a sensation so excruciating she feared her little heart would stop beating. Her soul was being strained out of her. Memories and emotions. Soon there'd be nothing left. Neither a human nor a bird.

"Sophia," the woman spoke in a honeyed voice. "Your friends are raising an army against me, are they?"

Twenty~One

BAILEY'S SLEEP HAD BEEN interrupted all night long by thoughts of his new kin keeping watch just outside his tent. He rose from his blankets, feeling the skin on his neck and arms tingling from the chilly, dense air. Outside the tent, rolling fog lit by the pink light of sunrise spread through the Allies' camp, which was tucked into the trees overlooking the valley. Two tigers lifted their heads and regarded him. He had spent the night in what seemed like a never-ending dream, his mind flitting from one tiger's consciousness to the next: he'd smelled the air and the dirt and the foreign sharpness of campfires just as they had; he'd felt their whiskers twitching at each nighttime noise as if their whiskers were his. He'd passed through their minds like a wanderer, always returning, in the end, to the mind of Taleth, like returning home at the end of a long journey.

Now he and Taleth walked together across the pine-needled

ground to Tremelo's tent. He was excited to show Tremelo the sword, which he'd clutched wordlessly the whole walk back after they'd been reunited. He was too happy and tongue-tied at the sight of more white tigers.

"I'm glad you're back, sir," Bailey said as he arrived at Tremelo's tent. There, he sat talking with Eneas, Digby, and Annika. When his teacher looked up, his expression was wary, as if he'd forced himself to smile. He rose from his seat.

"I am too. But I'm afraid our celebration is short-lived." There was a silence that followed, and Bailey looked behind him. The embers of Tremelo's campfire still glowed—he'd been awake all night long.

"Reconnaissance has announced that Viviana's army is on the move toward the school. I've consulted with the team," he said, motioning to Annika, Digby, and Eneas. "We agree it's best to march to the Seers' Valley and cut her off from the Peaks."

"Destroy her mines, too!" Digby added. "The Clarke fella told us the location."

"The location of what?" Gwen asked, holding up a flap of the tent in the threshold. She had a crease in her forehead and wore something like a frown, despite all of them being reunited again.

"Hello, Gwen," Tremelo said. It occurred to Bailey that they hadn't spoken last night when the two camps came together.

"Hello," Gwen said stiffly.

"Is this the headquarters of this operation?" Herman said, poking his head in over Gwen's. He must've followed Bailey there.

"Dad, this is Tremelo—Tremelo, this is my dad," Bailey said. "They've made the decision to march."

Gwen moved out of the way to let Herman pass, though she

didn't dare enter herself. The two men met in the middle of the tent and shook hands, nodding solemnly. "I'd be honored to march with the True King," Herman said.

"And I'd be honored by your service," Tremelo responded. "Shall we march?"

After a tearful good-bye with his mother, Bailey marched along-side his friends and his father toward the Velyn Peaks. Nearly half the camp had stayed at Fairmount under the watchful eye of Mrs. Copse. The warriors had allowed several students, including most of the Scavage team, to march and help carry supplies. They'd been on the trail for hours, a collective determination driving them forward up the mountain. Very little was said, and occasionally Bailey's dad would lift him up into a hug—which half embarrassed Bailey and half pleased him. It was good to combine the world of family and friends, even if Gwen was acting a bit strange. He guessed she was still angry over their disagreement the night before. But if he was being honest, he was a little bit angry too. There was a part of him that was glad Tremelo had proved them all wrong by coming back. The marchers stopped in a clearing near a valley and set up camp for the night. Bailey had put his pack down, and headed over to find his dad.

"Look!" Gwen said, grabbing his arm as he passed her. She was pointing up at the sky. Annika, Eneas, and Digby were nearby and listened in.

"Something's coming," she said. "Can you hear that?"

Bailey listened: he heard screeching in the near distance, from the direction of the valley below them. A huge flock of what sounded like birds was headed their way.

"The trees are too thick here to see them before they're directly over us," said Eneas. "I'll send a lookout down the hill."

"Look!" said Gwen, pointing up. One lone bird swooped into view, ahead of the screeching that was steadily growing louder. Bailey's breath caught in his chest as he recognized the familiar brown speckled feathers.

"It's Carin," said Gwen.

"Phi must be with her!" said Bailey. "That's my friend's kin familiar," he told his father. He looked up into the sky, waiting to see Phi in her new form.

Carin flapped over the camp, zigzagging between branches. She screeched.

"No—something's wrong," said Gwen.

From the trees behind Carin came the sound of hundreds of wings rushing toward the campsite. Bailey stared, openmouthed, as birds of every species poured across the sky and then circled overhead. Tori and Hal ran over from their tent.

"What are they doing?" asked Tori, staring up at the birds. "Are they here to help us?"

Carin landed next to them on a low branch. She squawked, shaking her feathers.

"No," said Gwen, looking from Carin to the sky. "I don't think so."

With a chaotic cry, the birds hastened their pace, as though something was chasing them. Gwen gasped and pointed upward. A shadow began to fall over the clearing as Viviana's giant Clamoribus, the one she'd used to fly away from the Progress Fair, glided into view above the treetops. Surrounding it were smaller Clamoribi, their metal wings moving in perfect synchronization.

Each of the individual Clamoribi opened their beaks, and Viviana's voice echoed out.

"Fighters of the so-called 'True King,' I address you now," her voice, multiplied through many mouths, began. "Your cause is nothing. Your 'king'? An insane traitor, begging for attention like a dog. You have no weapons that can stand against those of the Dominae. If you surrender now, I will be merciful. If you stand with your quivering insect of a king, you will be crushed."

The live birds began to circle over the trees. Their wings started beating the air in perfect precision, just like the Clamoribi.

"She's controlling them!" said Hal.

On the ground, several dogs traveling with the RATS began to howl and pace, and a number of rodents scattered from the campsites and into the underbrush. Next to Bailey, Taleth twitched her whiskers, growling. Every man and woman in the camp looked upward as the giant Clamoribus and its entourage passed over them.

The sound of shouting caused Bailey to turn his gaze back to the trees—several Velyn ran up the hill from the ravine, holding their weapons closely.

"Soldiers!" one shouted, a strong-shouldered man with a dark-brown beard. He held an axe. "Hundreds of them in formation in the valley!"

"No," gasped Gwen. "No, it's too soon—we're not ready!"

"We'll have to figure it out on the fly, then. . . ." Tremelo said. "Annika, what's the position of the archers? And Digby, Eneas, what's the report on the ground?"

"I have enough archers to join with the Velyn's along the cliff's edge overlooking the valley," she said. "And we have some cannon fire left as well. We'll position the ship at the edge of the ravine, below the archers."

"The Velyn are prepared," Eneas said.

"And the RATS are at the ready, the scrappy bunch," Digby added.

"But the animals..." Tremelo trailed off. "Have they been commanded to stay back? The Halcyon pieces were abandoned in the tunnels; we have no way of protecting our animals against Dominance."

Bailey sensed the tigers gathered just beyond the trees, their whiskers twitching. They bared their teeth as the Clamoribi floated away, back to the valley. Their hackles were raised, and several of them were confused by urges not their own.

"We can't let the animals fight," Bailey said. "Not until we know they'll be safe."

"You won't be fighting, either," said Herman, pointing to Bailey. "You're staying here while we forge ahead."

"Wait, what do you mean I can't fight?" called Bailey.

He looked back to Tremelo, who shared a look with Herman. "Your father is right. We need you alive," he said. "Who would follow the king who let a child—the Child of War, no less—die in battle? And that's exactly what would happen, if you go out there with us."

Bailey's hand curled into a fist around the hilt of the sword. His dad took a knee in front of him. "Your mom and I—we can't lose you, Bailey."

"You won't!" Bailey argued. "Let me come with you. I can help!" He raised his sword as if it were evidence.

"I'll fight for the both of us. I love you," his dad said as he pulled Bailey into a hug. He hugged his dad back, even if his own anger hadn't totally melted away. "Stay off the battlefield and out of sight."

"Fine," he said stiffly while his dad still hugged him. "And I love you too," he added in a mumble. His dad pulled away and mussed his sandy-colored hair before joining Tremelo, who'd turned toward the warriors.

"You still have the amulets?" Tremelo asked. When Bailey nodded he looked relieved. "Nature willing they add some protection. Stay safe, you lot!" He started to turn, but Bailey stopped him.

"Wait!" he called out, looking down at the sword in his hand.

Gwen gasped. "What are you doing?"

But Bailey ignored her. "Since I'm not going to be on the front lines, you should take this," he said as he lifted the handle toward Tremelo. "It belonged to your father, and it's powerful. I don't know how to explain it, but it's like it sings. Can you feel it?"

"Where did you—"

"Let's move," Eneas called from the distance.

Tremelo nodded at the Velyn warrior as he took the sword from Bailey. A sense of recognition passed over his eyes. "We'll save the story for after the battle. But it's true—I can feel it. Thank you, Bailey."

"Good luck, my king," Bailey said back.

"Let's find Shonfield, then," said Hal once the warriors had left them.

Bailey didn't answer. Instead, he turned back toward his tent. The others followed.

"Oh Nature, Bailey!" said Gwen. "What did you do that for?"

"Do what?" Bailey asked. He felt confused and frustrated.

"Why did I give our king a prophesized sword? So he could defeat Dominance!"

"But—"

"But what?" he asked, cutting her off. "You've been acting weird about Tremelo this whole time, and I don't know why."

"It's because of my visions. I . . ." She trailed off, her forehead wrinkled like she was searching for the right words. "I just need you to be careful."

Bailey's heart dropped down into the pit of his stomach. She hadn't been a Seer for very long, and he'd only just found out she was having visions. "Tremelo was in it?" he asked.

"Bailey, come quick!" Hal called from the trees below. He and Tori were hidden in the trees, perched to watch the battle from afar.

"You have to keep your distance from him," she whispered fiercely, grabbing on to his shoulders. She was a few inches taller, and he had to look up into her wide eyes. "Just until the battle is over."

"What did you see?" Bailey asked, his voice shaking.

"BAILEY! GWEN!" Tori yelled from below. "Get down here, already! It's Phi."

Gwen gave out a yelp and shot down the slope without another word. Bailey was on her heels, scrambling down the steep hill away from the camp. When they reached Hal and Tori, Bailey skidded on a patch of muddy earth, stopping short at a large, long boulder overlooking the valley. The others spread out alongside him and stared out over the rocky landscape.

"Ants alive," he breathed.

The Dominae filled the floor of the valley in line upon line of black-armored fighters. Soldiers holding swords and bayonets stood at the front—many, many lines back were soldiers on horse-back, next to some riding on saddled bears and lions. The animals stared directly ahead; no tails lashed or manes twitched. It looked like there were thousands upon thousands of soldiers down there.

"Where's Phi?" he asked.

Gwen clutched Bailey's arm tightly.

"There!" she said, as if her breath had been knocked out of her. She pointed across the battlefield to where Viviana's tents had been erected. Their white canvas snapped and waved in the wind, and as a loose tent flap changed direction, it revealed a figure of a falcon thrashing in the wind. It was tied down, and Bailey knew from the way it moved, fierce and defiant, that it was her.

Twenty~Two

AT THE SIGHT OF her, Bailey felt his knees buckle beneath him. Her ankle was bound in front of her, and a sharp-jawed woman dressed in Dominae black stood guard over her.

"Oh, *ants*," breathed Tori. "I hadn't believed Lukas until now. What can we do?"

"Tremelo needs to know," said Gwen.

"He's about to have a lot on his hands right now," said Hal.

Hundreds of the black metal steeds emerged from the forest, just like the one Clarke had ridden into the Dark Woods. Their eyes burned bright red, and tiny licks of flame shot out from their manufactured nostrils.

The four friends gaped as the Allied fighters began to appear directly below them. On a rock ledge just a few yards beneath their hiding place, the archers lined up, made up of men and women from the Velyn, the RATS, and from Defiance. At the bottom of the cliff, a ship rumbled into view, its cannons ready to fire. And finally, the fighters on foot. Tremelo stood with Digby, Eneas, and Bailey's dad.

"Look!" said Gwen, pointing to the center of the Dominae's forces. The soldiers stepped aside to form a pathway down the middle of the valley. Riding on a massive black metal horse was Viviana. Two Clamoribi flanked her, flying just a few feet over her head as she reached the front line of her troops, but Bailey saw that Tremelo didn't dare move.

"We'll have to save Phi ourselves," said Bailey from their perch.

"You promised your dad you wouldn't go!" Gwen said. "We can do it without you."

"But it's *Phi*," he told Gwen as he surveyed the distance between them and her—a sunken field now crisscrossed with flying arrows and the occasional blast and smoke of cannon fire. "You'll need all the help you can get."

"Then promise me you'll stay away from Tremelo," she begged. "Promise me!"

"What's going on?" Tori asked. She and Hal looked at them with worried expressions.

"There's no time to explain," she told them. Bailey didn't know himself. What had Gwen seen? But they were out of time, and he agreed just the same.

"Okay, I promise."

To reach Phi, they would have to skirt around the edge of the valley, out of sight on top of the ravine. If they tried to cross the field, they'd have no chance of getting to her without being captured themselves. But the edge of the valley was where Viviana's camp was stationed.

"Hal, find Taylor!" Bailey called. "Tell him to bring as many of the Scavage team as he can." This would be the game of a lifetime, he thought as he climbed down a steep, rocky ravine overlooking the narrow end of the battlefield. Gwen, Taylor, Arabella, two Blue Squad Squats, and Hal and Tori brought up the rear. Taleth paced back and forth on the rocks at the top of the ravine, and her anxiety bled into Bailey's.

"We don't have a Sneak," said Arabella. "*Phi's* our best Sneak."

Bailey clung to a moss-covered rock, only a few yards away from the valley floor. "Who should we send?" he asked.

"You," Taylor said in a way that made it sound like it was the most obvious answer. "You're faster than anyone here, even me."

"Make a decision already," said Arabella, behind them. "In case you didn't get the memo, Phi is a *bird*! Let's get moving."

So they did. Bailey couldn't wait to get on solid ground; the brush-covered cliffside they were now traversing was slippery under their feet.

"To the imposter leading this *army*," Viviana said, her voice booming from down below. She'd broken the silence first, Bailey thought as he and his friends scaled down the cliff. As he concentrated on his footing, he saw out of the corner of his eyes that the Clamoribi flew higher, amplifying her voice for the entire battlefield to hear.

"You risk the lives of your believers," she continued. "But you can avoid the spilling of their blood today." She paced on her metal horse in front of her troops. "Surrender yourself to me."

"He can't give himself up," whispered Gwen, in a strained breath. She crawled down a moss-covered rock and was much faster than Bailey would've guessed.

Tremelo took a step forward toward Viviana, and hundreds of Dominae archers that made up her front line aimed their drawn arrows at him in unison. Bailey paused, stopping in his tracks as he held his breath.

"Viviana," Tremelo said, shouting so loud that Bailey could hear him from where he stood. The True King didn't need the Clamoribi to speak. "I would sooner die."

Behind Tremelo, the Allies sent up a roaring cheer, holding their bows and swords and axes in the air. Bailey looked toward the tents and strained his eyes to catch another glimpse of Phi. Then he started scaling down double time.

Viviana sat tall on her metal horse. "Very well, then," she said. "Archers, FIRE!"

The soldiers for Tremelo shielded him with their makeshift armor as arrows were let loose. Shouts echoed across the valley as Viviana retreated back into the folds of her dark army, who closed ranks behind her.

The battle had begun and now raged down on them: the Defiance ships had come equipped with not only three cannons, but an impressive catapult that the Allies used to launch enormous boulders into the fray, scattering several of the Dominae at a time. The air above the valley was thick with flying arrows.

"Come on, Bailey," Tori said just below him.

They'd finally reached a narrow ledge that was just one long jump from the valley floor. One by one, they stealthily leapt down and immediately rolled behind a flank of bushes. From here, they could see the backs of Viviana's last line of defense, mounted on their metal steeds. Viviana's tent stood several yards away, guarded by four Dominae solders, all in black uniforms, with peaked helmets and the insignia of the hand and claw on their chests. Outside of the tent sat two figures tied with ropes to a tree—a thin, ashen-skinned man who hid his face in his bent knees, and Phi.

"Okay, listen up," said Taylor, sounding every bit the squad captain. "We all know what we're doing, then? Arabella, you'll lead your Squats out behind me and Bailey, while the Slammers distract. And bench squad—Hal, Tori, redhead—you'll provide the cover up here from the rocks."

Hal and Tori nodded. Gwen nervously lowered her gaze to the ground.

"If you get in trouble, just *run*," Taylor continued. "We're the fastest team in Aldermere, and the best at hiding too. Don't let anyone corner you, know where your best chance at an exit is, and you'll be all right." He nodded at Bailey, who felt a lump the size of an orange rise in his throat. What if, he thought, they wouldn't be all right after all?

"Okay," Bailey said, swallowing his fear. "Let's go."

"Wait!" Gwen pulled Bailey back by his sleeve. Her eyes were red and wide. "I have to tell you. What Clarke said about the horses, and the strange animals—I saw it. My vision was exactly how he described it. I was running from a shiny, metal horse. . . . It breathed fire." She put her face in her palms, took a deep breath, and kept going. "It was going to kill me. And I thought I'd outrun it, but then there were other animals. Real animals. They moved strangely, with a vacant look in their eyes."

"We're going to take care of each other!" Bailey assured her. "We're going to get Phi, and we're going to stay together. You'll be safe, I promise."

"But I'm not just worried about me. I'm worried about *you*!"

She crossed her arms tightly. "You need protecting too. And how am I supposed to be of any help? At the battle with Sucrette, I had the harmonica. Now, I can't even get one owl to come near me! And if the kin are Dominated, or worse—"

The Allies had done their best to send their kin away, but the trees surrounding the sunken gorge were filled with birds of every flock, and the underbrush shook with the anxious bodies of rodents and canines called by their bonds to watch what unfolded. The Allies could no more keep their kin from coming than a patch of grass could stop a sea tide. Bailey knew that it was only a matter of time before Viviana would use this to her advantage—but he hoped that he and his friends could take one desperate chance before that happened. He hoped that Gwen could.

Bailey turned back to face her, straightening up. She was upset, that much was clear—but what could he say at a moment like this? He thought of Phi, and wondered what she would do. The answer was she'd listen to Gwen. She'd try to understand why she was scared.

"You're scared we won't all make it?" he asked.

She nodded. "I'm scared of what's going to happen on that battlefield. . . ."

He grabbed her shoulders gently, and she looked up. Her eyes were wet with tears.

"We're doing this for Phi," Bailey said. "And for Tremelo, and for all of Aldermere. Maybe . . . let yourself feel the fear and really give in to it."

"Feel the fear?" Gwen wiped her eyes. "How?"

"I don't know," Bailey admitted. "When I first got to Fairmount I was so scared—of what the other kids would think, or that I'd never Awaken. And even though my bond is still new, it grew strong so fast. I think it was because Taleth and I had each other, and we weren't as scared anymore. And because I have new friends—like you. And Phi and Hal and Tori. I don't feel so alone. I don't fear what'll come next. And somehow that makes the bond stronger. Maybe you could try to focus on what you have?" He couldn't do it justice, couldn't explain it any better than that. But it seemed to be enough for Gwen.

"I'll try," she said. "But, Bailey, you have to come right back after Phi is free. Come right back so we can all look out for each other."

He nodded. "And I almost forgot," he said as he pulled one of the metal amulets out of his pocket. "Take this."

Together, they peered at the imposing line of soldiers just a few paces away, all with their backs turned to them. Bailey took a deep breath.

"I'll meet you on the other side of the rocks," he said to Gwen, Hal, and Tori—who stayed at the rocks for now. Bailey and the Scavage team would push forward, while his friends would run around the perimeter to help secure Phi. Hopefully he'd make enough of a commotion that no one would notice them.

He made sure that the tiger's claw was secure in his belt, and he crept away, skirting the rocks at the cliff's bottom, around the edge of the battlefield. He stopped at a patch of shrewsberry bushes just a few feet from the rear of Viviana's tent. Phi sat with watchful eyes looking out at the battle, so close Bailey could throw a pebble at her feet. He twisted his head so that he could see Taylor peering back at him from behind the bushes. Bailey nodded, a gesture that Taylor returned before turning back to the others waiting closer to the cliff face. Bailey hunkered down behind the bush, took a deep breath, and closed his eyes.

He couldn't stop thinking about Gwen, and how afraid she was that her bond was irreparably broken. He was frightened too. To free Phi, he and his friends were all risking their lives, and they had nothing to help them but the bond. If his friends weren't able to place their trust in it, then nothing was certain.

Bailey searched the woods atop the ravine for Taleth's mind. To find her, he focused on the sound of the wind whisking the topmost branches of the evergreens—a sound barely audible from where he crouched close to the battle. But where Taleth stood, hidden in the dense growth overlooking the ravine, it was as loud as thunder. Bailey felt her ears twitch. A dew-covered bush left a streak of moisture on Taleth's left flank as she prowled closer to the edge of the ravine.

From there, she—and he—could see Tori, Hal, and Gwen. They stood closely together in a row, with Tori in the middle. Through Taleth's eyes, Bailey watched them join hands.

"Okay, Taleth," Bailey whispered, nearly knocking himself out of her mind at the strange sound of his own voice. "We're going to help them now."

Taleth began to purr, a sensation that filled Bailey with warmth. As both himself and the tiger, he focused all his energy on his friends. He and Taleth remembered together what it had been like to feel them, to feel their bonds working. It had been as though every human's bond was Bailey's too, joining onto his and making it stronger and more beautiful. He and Taleth breathed, and Bailey imagined a shimmering golden rope, stretching from Taleth to Tori, Hal, and Gwen.

Just as that rope seemed tautest, Taleth's mind slipped Bailey, without warning, into a memory. As it had before, the sudden change of the trees and sounds unnerved Bailey. But he kept breathing, reminding himself to stay with Taleth, or be shaken from the bond. He calmed himself and took stock of where—and when—he was. Taleth was in the mountains again, but farther south, where the trees gave way to rocks, and the bushes to prickly, weather-hardy moss. Bailey heard the cry of a tiny creature: a human infant. It lay on the ground in front of Taleth, wrapped in a wide piece of blond mountain lion fur. It looked up past Taleth, reaching its stubby hands out toward something just out of Taleth's vision.

Take him down the mountain, said a voice. Bailey sensed a woman standing just behind Taleth. Her hand rested on the tiger's back as Bailey realized that the woman had, in actuality, said nothing. Taleth had merely understood her thoughts. *Leave him someplace safe. I trust you, Taleth,* thought the woman, her voice filling Taleth's mind with pure, clear intention. *I know you won't fail me. Don't be afraid.* Taleth turned away from the crying child and looked at the woman. She was backlit by sunlight, but Bailey saw matted curls of long hair, and the glint of light reflecting off a teary cheek. Taleth rubbed her head against the woman's waist and began to purr.

Bailey fought through the haze of Taleth's memories to return his sight to the present—to his friends standing on the rocks. The loving voice of the woman in Taleth's mind echoed in Bailey's too. *I know you won't fail me. Don't be afraid.*

He squeezed the metal amulet in his palm. The powerful hum

he felt in Taleth's chest was as familiar to him now as his own breath. Their bond grew in intensity, filling his mind with warmth. As he focused on the clasped hands of Tori, Gwen, and Hal, Bailey knew that they were beginning to feel their bonds strengthen too. Tori and Hal seemed almost to glow as their bonds to the snakes and bats in the surrounding woods began to stir and to gather. Only Gwen's bond remained small and fragile, like a candle flame between two bonfires. Bailey wished he could speak directly to her. *I trust you,* he'd have said. *I know you won't fail.*

The ground under Taleth's paws began to quiver with movement. Snakes, hundreds of them, slithered under cover of fallen leaves and around the intrusive shapes of raised roots to the edge of the rocks. Taleth didn't move, and neither did Bailey. Bailey looked up—and suddenly he was looking up from the floor of the gorge again, solidly back in his own body—just in time to see the whooshing levy of bats burst from behind the treetops. They swirled in descent, mirroring the progression of the vast assemblage of snakes slithering down the face of the cliff, all converging on the battlefield. Bailey scanned the crowded sky for the third species he'd expected to see, but there were no owls in sight.

"You can do it, Gwen," Bailey whispered. "I *know* you can." He thought about the first battle they'd all fought together, against the duplicitous Miss Sucrette. Gwen had been fearless then: her owls, powered by her harmonica music and her own unshakeable faith in the bond, had helped bring Sucrette down. Now seeing Dominance grow so powerful had eroded that confidence, but Bailey knew that Gwen could find it again. She *had* to.

A black snake with yellow stripes sped over Bailey's right

foot and toward the battle. Its kin were already out there, winding around the ankles of the Dominae soldiers and whisking past their stomping heels. The soldiers broke ranks as they tried to wave the swarming bats away from their helmets.

Taylor lifted his hand straight up in the air and made a gesture like a countdown. At the final flick of his fingers, Arabella and the two Squats emerged from the bushes, positioned several yards apart. The three Scavage players ran headlong into the soldiers' camp in three different directions like clanking cannonballs. Arabella was the loudest of the three: "What's this?!" she shouted, as the soldiers still struggled to fight their way through the mess of snakes and bats. "There's a student here! Better catch her!" She and the others drew the Dominae away from the tent where Phi sat, providing a clear path between Phi and the safety of the cliff-side. Each time the soldiers tried to tackle or overtake the Scavage players, the bats swarmed in front of them, or the snakes impeded their way. Beside the tent, the soldier guarding Phi stepped away from her to wave some especially eager bats from his face.

"You're up," said Taylor.

Bailey felt for the curved tiger's claw in his belt as he watched his teammates draw the Dominae soldiers away from the captives. He took a deep breath and stood up. On the rocks, Gwen stood too. Their eyes met, and he nodded. She looked stricken—her bond was weak, as she had told him. But she had one other task that didn't require the bond at all. Upon seeing Bailey's nod, she placed two fingers in her mouth and whistled:

Whit whit whoo!

And then Gwen took off, scrambling down the rocks and charging toward Phi. Bailey tried to see if Phi had heard the whistle, but his view was blocked by a cloud of bats. Gwen whistled again as she ran.

The bats swerved, and Bailey's breath caught in his throat—Phi was struggling, flapping frantically and tethered to a pole by a leather strap. It was her. He made a run for it, ready to cut the strap with the tiger claw he clutched with his hand.

Twenty-Three

TIME SLOWED. PHI'S SHARP eyes took in the sight of Bailey and Tremelo in danger, and the haze of Dominance fell away. She remembered how she'd gotten here, and who she was. She was a bird and a girl, straddling two worlds—and right now her friends needed her, because she had the key to defeating Viviana's army.

At the thought of Carin, her friends, her family, those she loved—it awoke something in her that resisted the Dominance. And not only that, but memories came flooding back to her. She remembered how she'd changed into a bird, and why she'd changed. Yet none of it mattered. These would be her last moments as a falcon and it didn't matter.

She closed her eyes and remembered the forsaking spell. She remembered the chant as the words formed before her, and she felt a sense of understanding. *Release me*, she thought. *I want to be a human again*—and suddenly her body was stretching and contorting. A reversal of what she'd wanted. Her talons elongating and fingers forming; her skull growing and her brain expanding; her body stretching. She felt all her organs contracting, growing— and the pain was so excruciating she thought she might implode. There was no way to live through this agony, no other side. And when she'd passed the point of no return, when she was certain the last sensation she'd feel was like a thousand knives cutting into her skin, the worn leather strap around her ankle tightened and burst.

Phi feared she would die. But she needed to tell her friends that there was a way to drive back the Dominance.

Her first words were the names of her two best friends.

"Bailey! Gwen!" she called out in her human voice. And when she saw their faces, she knew it was worth it. Even if she could never shift back to her falcon form, being here was worth it.

Twenty~Four

BAILEY TORE HIS EYES away just as Phi transformed back into her human form. Out of the corner of his eye he saw her tear away the piece of the white canvas tent and cover herself as she broke into a run. Gwen grabbed her hand and pulled her off to the side of the battle. Before she disappeared into the trees, she stole a glance at Bailey and nodded once. It warmed his heart with triumph.

They ran to the cover of nearby trees and scrambled back up the ravine.

"Look at that," said Taylor. He pointed to the treetops at the far edge of the ravine. In the sky, the black outlines of birds flew overhead.

"What is it?" asked Hal, running up alongside them. Tori was at his side, and all of them squinted at the cloudy sky.

"It's people's kin," said Tori. "They're not Dominated, though. Not yet."

A rustle to their left caused them to gasp; out of the under-growth ran a herd of brown and white rabbits. They dashed to the rocks and then began hopping down along the steep cliff face, into the ravine. Bailey leaned over the rock and saw that a pack of wolves had already joined the Allies on the battlefield, despite the Velyn's attempts to keep them out of the Dominae's reach. Other forest creatures appeared at the foot of the cliffs, drawn by the adrenaline of their human kin.

"They'll only become weapons," Bailey said. He sensed the tigers back at camp, pacing relentlessly among the tents, flashing their teeth at the sounds of fighting happening just yards away. They stayed where they were, but other animals began to appear on the rocks and from behind the trees, watching the battle unfold just like Bailey and his friends.

"I don't know about that," said Tori, pointing through the bushes to the field. "Look at the animals fighting in the front lines."

The two armies clashed at the foot of the cliff face, and though Bailey expected to see each rabbit, fox, badger, and more that had joined the Allies falling prey to Dominance, they were fighting alongside the Allies, advancing on the Dominae with no sign of being controlled. While the front lines clashed, however, the animals inside the perimeter of the fire horses stood still, unblinking.

Bailey showed his friends what he saw; Hal and Tori nodded as the realization dawned.

"It's like the machines are controlling how far the Dominance can go," Gwen said.

"But we saw what happened at the Fair," said Tori. "Viviana could control this whole valley if she wanted. Why would she limit her power now?"

Bailey scanned the battlefield; past the flank of fire horses, riding on her own mechanical charge, sat Viviana. He remembered the trace of panic in her demeanor when the Reckoning had grown beyond her restraint.

"She's afraid of herself," he whispered. "She lost control at the Fair."

"That may be," said Hal. "But she's also *more* powerful if she reins in the Dominance like this."

Bailey and the others looked at Hal. After a moment, Tori gasped.

"Of course!" she said. "It's just like the orbs. The energy of the Dominance, when it's contained, can react to itself. It builds power."

"Right," said Hal. "So horses are like the walls of the orbs."

Bailey stared at the unmoving soldiers within the Dominae's core, and shuddered. The Allies had a fighting chance as long as their animal kin were outside that perimeter, but he hated to think what might happen if they actually fought their way through. Their side didn't have enough orbs to ward them off. And all the kin who had joined in the fray would be at the mercy of the Dominae. The Allies wouldn't stand a chance.

"Guys, we have trouble!" Tori said. The fire horses were unleashed onto the crowd. In the distance he saw one of the horses advancing on his father from behind. Its rider fought at the torrent of kin, but the eyes of the fire horse were focused, unwavering, on Herman.

"DAD!" Bailey called out just as Taleth roared. His dad turned a split second too late; Bailey saw his body slammed down to the ground. He lost sight of his dad and his adrenaline spiked. He slid down the rocks, hopped over two animals pawing viciously at one another, and sidestepped archers and soldiers who fought the Allies. There was a cloud of feathers and claws blocking his view; the kin were frantic.

He was vaguely aware of Gwen calling to him, but he could only focus on reaching his dad. He saw the Tully and a group of women overtake the horse who had attacked his dad. Then two women heaved up his dad's body, and Bailey saw his dad could not lift his head. His clothes were covered with blood.

Around him he saw that many other kin, however, appeared to be swirling back against their will, pulled by the Dominae's growing force. Bailey grabbed the tiger's claw from his belt and hacked at a vulture who attempted to swoop down at him. The claw tore through its chest and it fell to the ground with a thud, flapping its wings violently. There was so much blood. It made him sick to his stomach.

Bailey reached his father and propped him up to sit. The Defiance women beat back the nearby possessed kin and Dominae soldiers, though the danger was immediate.

"I'm going to get you out of here," Bailey assured him.

"I know you will," his dad said, trying to smile. He cradled his right side as if he'd broken an arm or a rib. He had bloody gashes all over his neck and chest, and his face was contorted with pain. Meanwhile, from where Bailey sat he could see the vulture he'd slashed; its movements were slowing, and it could barely flap its wings. It was as if he'd ripped a gash in his own chest. The agony he felt watching it struggle was overwhelming. I've taken its life, he thought when it finally lay still.

But just as soon as he thought it, the vulture lifted its head and scanned the area until it locked its eyes on Bailey.

"No," Bailey whispered. He was certain the bird had died; he'd felt the life drain out of it. Yet now it extended its wings so that Bailey could see its bloodied chest in full glory. It jumped up in the air and dove toward him.

Cutting through the air, it extended its talons and tried to claw at his face—but one of the Defiance warriors stepped between them and brought a pan up and over, smashing the bird down before it had reached them. It was Myra, the woman he'd met once they crossed the canyon.

"Thank you!" he breathed.

"Behind you!" she yelled.

Bailey spun around, the claw in his hand—but it was a metal horse, and against that he was practically defenseless. Myra ran to his side and lifted the pan up once more, but it would do no more good than his own weapon.

As the steed reared back on its hind legs, snorting flames from its welded nostrils, Bailey tucked his head down into his dad's chin. He waited for the heat, for a fire that would burn him with his dad in his arms—but instead his ears rang with a high, long note not unlike music. He looked up and saw Tremelo, swinging the sword up toward the horse with all his strength. Bailey expected sparks to fly as the steel of the sword met the silver enamel of the horse's neck—but they didn't. Instead, the sword met no resistance at all, slicing cleanly through the fire horse as if it were slicing through a piece of wobbly custard in the Fairmount dining hall. The rider let out a yelp of surprise and fell backward as his steed's metal head went sliding, then crashing, down to the ground.

The pure sound hung in the air. It seemed to be coming from the sword. Then he noticed that the birds and bats who had clouded his vision before were now giving him a wide berth. In fact, they circled him in a perfect formation, but from several feet away on all sides. Gliding and dipping, they seemed to echo the sound of the sword with their movements, participating in a dance that only they could understand, but that Bailey felt growing inside of him too. The song of the sword was protecting them and their bonds.

Bailey whirled around, meaning to thank Tremelo. But his teacher had lifted the sword over his head once more. The way he held it was unnatural, as though it were against his will—and he had a pained look on his face.

"Bailey, run—" he managed to say in a strained voice.

Myra and the other warriors were now fighting off soldiers and the reanimated kin. Behind him, at the top of the hill, the true force of the Dominae army stood silhouetted against the pink-streaked clouds: an impenetrable formation of fire horses, with a mass of dead-eyed beasts behind them. They would never stop coming.

Then, Bailey saw the mounted figure on the rocks behind his mentor: Viviana was watching them. Ash from the mouth of her fire horse swirled in the air around her, mixing with the ash from the other horses that had followed her down the riverbed. They stood in a loose formation, each one only yards away from him. He and Tremelo sat inside Viviana's web. Everything seemed to Bailey to be taking place in slow motion: he looked up at the cloudy sky, and saw several birds flying around him and Tremelo in a perfect, uniform circle. A horde of foxes, rabbits, and other kin were creeping on all fours or slithering from the woods, joining in the slow, meticulous circle as they neared where Tremelo stood. They watched Bailey with lifeless eyes.

Taleth stirred, and lowered herself in the distance—as if she was ready to break into a sprint. Bailey couldn't tell who she'd attack or what she was thinking. Viviana's influence was blocking him. He remembered what Clarke said, that Viviana and her metal steeds were impossible to defeat. That they were tainted, evil, and fed off of fear. But Bailey couldn't accept it.

"Tremelo," Bailey whispered as he clutched the orb in his hand. He kept his eyes on Tremelo's fists. "Don't be afraid. You can resist this—you can resist *her.*"

"Surrender to it!" Viviana called out. She wore armor made of the same silver-enameled metal as her horse. The flickers of flame from its nose reflected in her breastplate.

The air around Bailey felt thick, as though he could actually sense the warping of the bond happening around him. Viviana's power radiated out from her, and then doubled back again as it reflected off the horses in the circle. It made Bailey's skin tingle and his hair stand on edge. Taleth lunged down from the rocks and ran toward them. The ash from the horses rose off the white rocks, buffeted not by wind but by an invisible electro-current that emanated from Viviana herself.

Tremelo lifted the sword. "But I am afraid," he said with a grunt.

Every muscle in Tremelo's face and neck seemed to shake with the effort of resisting Viviana. Bailey glanced to his side: the possessed animals circled in closer—he couldn't escape without them tearing him to pieces.

"I'm not," Bailey said. And it was true. He'd worried about the people he loved, and the fate of the kingdom, but his faith in Tremelo had never wavered. He was their king. He believed in the bond. There was no one in all of Aldermere more fit for the job of repairing what they'd damaged through Dominance. The book of prophecies told him he was the Child of War, but only now did he know what it meant. It meant to prevent wars, and to remind people that their bonds would overcome the darkness.

Tremelo lifted the sword higher and made a ragged sound halfway between a breath and a cry. Bailey closed his eyes as the song of Melore's sword rang out. He heard Gwen scream and felt Taleth's anger. He tried to hold steady to this feeling of unshakable faith, but it was harder and harder the closer Taleth came—the tiger was preparing to lunge.

Twenty~Five

TREMELO LOWERED THE SWORD just as Taleth slid to a stop a few feet behind them. "I'm sorry. I'm so sorry. My hands—they weren't my own. It was almost as if the sword was helping me, though. It wouldn't let me give in." He looked at it with wonder.

"The sword didn't resist her Dominance. You did," Bailey said.

"Horses! Formation!" Viviana called from the rocks. Even from here Bailey could feel her anger, and the heat of her stare.

Tremelo stood tall to survey the ring of fire horses that surrounded them. The horses and their riders were closing in. "They're creating a circuit," he said. "We must flee."

"But my dad's been hurt," Bailey said as he looked down at Herman in his arms.

Tremelo knelt down and looked into Herman's eyes, and the two men nodded solemnly at each other. "We're going to get you two to safety," Tremelo told him. He eased his shoulder under Herman's arm as if to help him walk. "Stay with me." Then he rushed Herman to the nearest edge of the circle and tried to evade a parade of Dominated animals—but they abruptly stopped their movements and began to follow him instead. At the edge, Tremelo plunged the sword into the flank of a fire horse with his free arm, then swung himself around with Herman in tow—"Duck, Bailey!"—and sliced off the head of the one next to it. The soldiers dismounted, panicked. Bailey looked back as Tremelo left the circle: the animals were now rushing toward them and the remainder of the horses plodded slowly, mechanically in their direction as well.

"They're following the sword!" Bailey said. "The bond is pulling them with us now!"

Together, the three of them half walked and half ran down the rocks. It was obvious that his dad was in pain. They went as far as the riverbed could take them, and came to an abrupt stop at its ending; what had surely once been a waterfall down the mountain was now nothing but a steep, high cliff. Bailey staggered as he looked down and saw the tops of trees many, many yards below. The clatter of metal hooves pounding the rocks echoed up to Bailey's ears.

"I think we should step back," his dad said. The ground underneath them began to shake. Bailey thought he heard someone call his name from the trees, but he couldn't tear his eyes away from the oncoming army. The stampeding metal horses reminded him of the dust storm he and his friends had endured in the Plains—menacing and unreal, like a mountain suddenly given the power to move. The fire horses charged across the rocks. Their red eyes gleamed. Behind them came all the animals whose lives had been taken in the battle, but whose bodies had been forced to keep fighting.

Tremelo stood at the edge of the cliff and planted his feet firmly on the rocks.

"Get close," he ordered. "Hold on to your father."

Bailey wrapped his arms around his dad's other side as Tremelo held Melore's sword high with his free hand. "Don't let go!" he said.

Suddenly, they were surrounded by fire and blackness.

"Bailey, I was afraid!" Tremelo yelled over the noise of animals that stampeded toward them. "I was afraid I couldn't be the king my father was."

"And now?" Bailey yelled back. He could barely hear himself as he held up his father. The animals were closing in.

"And now I know I won't be the same kind of king. I'll be my own king. Knowing that makes me less afraid."

Just then the horse stampede arrived and split around them like water around a river's stone. The contraptions leapt into the chasm below. Stumbling, the wounded, mangled animals that had no life left in them except Viviana's will came charging after the ponies, drawn by the hum of the sword. The kin were still Dominated, but the sword created a barrier of protection—a safe bubble in which they could stand without fear.

The animals swarmed around Bailey and followed the horses to their final rest. The current in the air snapped around the sword. Bailey felt the Dominae's power draining away as Tremelo's grew stronger. When finally the last of the metal steeds had launched themselves off the cliff, Bailey let go of Tremelo. Breathless, they peered over the edge. All they could see was a black cloud of ash that rose up the cliff and unfurled over them.

Bailey's dad slumped to the ground.

"Dad, are you okay?" he asked, crouching down next to him.

"I'm fine, Bailey—just a little scratched up and overwhelmed, is all." But Bailey thought he was a lot more than scratched up. Now as his jacket fell open, Bailey saw he'd been trampled on his left side by the metal horse, and could barely move his left arm or even walk.

"Bailey! Tremelo! Mr. Walker!" Gwen, Phi, Tori, and Hal called to them from the pines, then ran down the sloping sides of the riverbank to join them. Phi wore an oversized tunic that the women of Defiance wore. Someone must've given it to her just after she'd transformed. She placed a hand over her heart as she looked down the cliff.

"Are you okay?" Bailey and Phi said in unison the moment they made eye contact.

"I'm okay now. But them—those poor creatures," cried Phi. "The animals."

"They're at peace now," Tremelo said, trying to offer some comfort.

Bailey pulled back from Phi. "This is my dad," he said to Phi, and Gwen, who now stood next to her. Herman smiled weakly at the girls from the ground. Phi put her hand up in a small wave, though her face was etched in worry. Gwen's too. Tori and Hal introduced themselves and sat down on either side of Herman.

The trees were then full of sound: birdsong and scuttled leaves as so many living animals emerged from the woods. Carin landed on a low branch, and Phi nodded at her. Bailey's heart grew warm as he sensed the tigers coming closer. He looked toward the Ally camp and saw the pack running between the pine trees toward him and his friends. Annika had just arrived and gave everyone a nod as she stood at Bailey's side.

"It's not over," Phi warned. She pointed up the riverbed, where the ash had yet to settle. Viviana made her way toward them on foot. When she passed through the cloud of black ash, her proud expression softened as soon as she laid eyes on Annika.

"Viv?" Annika said.

For a moment, Viviana looked thoughtful, and Bailey saw the resemblance between her and Tremelo. It was the same look he'd had so many times in the past, when the man was trying to describe the mechanics of his newest invention, or when he talked about the bond.

But Viviana's face hardened, and Bailey saw sparks bouncing off of her hands and hair. Her power flashed, weak and chaotic, but still alive.

"I don't need anyone to tell me who I am," she called. "I'm the queen of Aldermere!" An electro-current static cracked around her and floated in the black dust.

"How are we supposed to stop her?" Tori said.

"I think I know a way," Phi answered. "No—I *know* I know a way. When I was a bird, I resisted her Dominance by remembering my friendships. My family. People who love me."

"Could it be that easy?" Hal said.

"I know it sounds easy, but there was something powerful

enough about those memories that I just snapped out of her spell. I had to relive those moments. . . ."

Out of the corner of his eye, Bailey saw many white shapes moving slowly, crouched, around him and Viviana. The tigers had come to join the fight. Viviana saw them too—she reached out with her right hand and sent a burst of ash, flashing like lightning, in the direction of the prowling tigers. One of them, a broad-nosed male, shook his head and stepped back. Dark-eyed, he approached Viviana like a faithful servant. The male tiger's presence in Bailey's mind extinguished like a spent candle.

"She still has her power!" he shouted. "We have to listen to Phi! It's worth trying."

"Annika has good memories with her, don't you?" Gwen asked. "And Tremelo!"

But Tremelo was no longer listening. He stepped forward and pleaded with her. "Viviana, listen to me!" he said. "You don't want this power—maybe you never have. You're afraid of it. Afraid of yourself. Let us help you. You could use the bond as we do, without hurting anyone. You don't have to be a creature of fear."

Viviana took a deep breath. Bailey remained focused on her face, and he swore he saw it soften, for a moment. But then, all too quickly, her violet eyes narrowed.

"Afraid?" she hissed. "How can I be afraid now? Everything has been taken from me. Even you, little brother." She flinched, and the male tiger leapt forward, its teeth and claws bared at Tremelo. Tremelo braced himself with the sword.

"No, don't hurt it!" Bailey cried. He couldn't bear to watch Tremelo kill one of his own kin. But something happened when the tiger came close to the sword: it growled and backed away.

"Damn you!" screamed Viviana. Another tiger plodded to her side, then another, and another. Bailey's hands shook as he sensed each one being overtaken by Viviana. Soon all of the white tigers stood at Viviana's side. She marched forward with the tigers flanking her.

The Allies had begun to return to the riverbed; they watched as Viviana advanced on Tremelo, using the tigers almost as guards. Tremelo, strengthened by the sword, could keep them at bay, but Viviana's Dominance was still powerful enough to drive him backward, straight over the cliff if she wanted.

"We have to do something," Phi urged.

Eneas and several more of the Velyn emerged from the pine woods and ran out onto the rocks. With him was yet one more white tiger. Puzzled, Bailey tried to think if he'd seen this one before; it felt different than the others to him. He couldn't sense its mind, but at the same time, he was certain that Viviana couldn't, either. It was acting on its own accord: its movements fast and instinctual, not at all like the empty, mechanical actions of the Dominated animals. Its blue eyes burned with inner life. When it saw Viviana, it began to run. It leapt, hurdling itself through the mass of its kin.

Viviana shielded herself with a dagger—she plunged it deep into the tiger's chest, and drops of its bright blood fell on the smooth white rock.

"NO!" Bailey cried. He pulled the two orbs out of his pocket and shoved one in Tremelo's hand. Gwen quickly found hers and handed it to Annika, while Bailey kept the third one for himself and made them hold hands.

"What is this about?" Annika asked.

"Bailey, I don't know if this will work! They're designed to—"

"*Shhh.* Just listen for a minute," he said. Then he called to Phi: "Tell us what to do!"

She grabbed on to Gwen's arm for support. "Everyone, think of a memory—a good one—of Viviana. A time when she showed you kindness!"

Bailey felt uncertain. He couldn't think of a moment when she'd showed him kindness, so he kept his mind blank and thought of Taleth. And then suddenly memories streamed through him—Annika's and Tremelo's—and they were powerful and charged with goodwill. There was Annika and Viviana as children in the Dust Plains, distributing water and helping other girls who trudged along in their chains. There was a little boy, Tremelo, being carried by Viviana after he'd fallen. His sister clutched him tightly as he tried not to cry, searching through the palace for King Melore himself—who swept them both into a hug. But there were many, many more. They were beautiful and full of joy. Vivana, the girl with the purple eyes, under a tree in the summertime. She wore a smile as she laid her head on the belly of a happy pig. Her kin.

"Oh Nature!" Viviana cried at the memory of her with her kin. It was the first time Bailey had ever heard her sound like what she once was—a little girl, afraid. She looked to Tremelo. "Brother! Help me!"

"It's weakening her," Tremelo yelled in a pained voice. But Annika clutched his hand even tighter.

"She must remember these moments. The past is painful."

"Please," Viviana pleaded once more. Then she dropped to the ground.

Tremelo ran to his sister and took her hand in his. The white tigers, now free, crowded around them both. "Is she alive?" Tremelo asked. "She knew me, in the end. You saw those memories. She's my family. Maybe we pushed her too far."

Bailey saw how pained Tremelo was. It was because he had faith in the bond, and saw the best in people, that he thought Viviana could've been saved.

"She needed to remember the girl, the woman, she was. The one with kindness, with a sense of justice . . ." Annika said behind them.

Taleth gave a mournful growl, and Bailey remembered the white tiger whom Viviana had hurt. It lay on the rocks, bleeding. Taleth rubbed her head against the wounded tiger's shoulder. Taleth looked at Bailey and roared—a short, desperate roar that tore at Bailey's heart. He tried to follow her thoughts, but they were saturated with feeling, with loss and fear and heavy, heavy love. The others, Bailey's friends and fellow warriors, began to gather around.

Then: a miracle. Viviana stirred. "Ollie," she whispered.

"Who's Ollie?" Hal asked, pushing up his glasses. Everyone had taken a step back, Bailey included.

"Ollie was her kin. Her friend and her kin," Tremelo said. "She remembered. . . ."

"What will you do?" Bailey asked Tremelo. He was still terrified of her, even if she lay barely conscious in her brother's arms.

"She'll stand trial. A fair trial."

One of the Velyn women came and took Viviana in her arms. "We'll see she's confined, and see to her health care in the meantime," she said. Bailey didn't think she deserved as much, but stopped himself from thinking such dark thoughts. Everyone deserved a trial and to be treated with humanity—even if they themselves weren't willing to do the same.

"The Dominae troops have scattered," announced Digby. "With their queen weakened and their metal trinkets dead, they're soft as dormice."

Phi and Gwen joined Bailey over the injured tiger.

"Eneas!" Bailey called, thinking of the Velyn's potent King's Fingers salve. "Eneas, help!"

To Bailey's surprise, Eneas stopped short when he saw the tiger lying on its side before him. He clutched a hand to his heart.

"Oh Nature," he said. "Not this."

"Can you help her?" Bailey asked.

Eneas shook his head. He rubbed his beard and looked at the tiger sadly.

"The salve can help ease her pain, but it cannot completely heal. If she were human ... our skin takes to the salve best. But I have asked her before ... and after so many years ..."

"What do you mean?" Bailey asked. "Asked who?"

Eneas knelt next to the tiger. He placed a careful hand on the side of its neck. The tiger blinked and breathed out in a huff, shaking its whiskers.

"My queen," Eneas whispered, "if you have any strength left, use it now."

"What are you saying?" asked Tremelo. "What is this creature?"

Eneas looked up and nodded toward the women from Defiance, who were now running to join them. He did not move his hand from the tiger's neck, but with his other hand, he pointed at the Tully.

"Ask her," he said. "This creature made a vow, and after so much time—too much time, I fear—I must ask her to break it."

Phi gasped. The Tully hastened to Eneas's side, breathing heavily.

"Is it her?" she cried.

Eneas placed his other hand on the tiger's forehead. It—she—closed her eyes at his touch. She shuddered; her fur shook.

Bailey felt Phi grab his hand.

"It's impossible," the Tully whispered. "Not after *years*."

Bailey could hardly comprehend what he saw happening in front of his very eyes. First, the tiger's body seemed to shrink and grow narrower. Her thick forepaws lengthened and thinned, and her claws disappeared. In their place, human fingers grasped at the cold earth, and lean, muscular arms reached out to the Tully, who clasped the creature's hand in her own. The fur melted away, and in its place Bailey saw human skin and a messy mane of long, curly hair the color of dark honey. The Tully pulled off her cloak and used it to cover the body of the woman who now lay where the tiger had been.

No one spoke—in fact, it seemed to Bailey as if every human and beast on the battlefield was holding its breath, watching. The air had gone still as death. Eneas bent over the woman, applying his salve to the wound in her side.

"Who is she?" asked Phi.

"Help me lift her," called Eneas, gesturing to Tremelo, whose face had gone white. Bailey had never seen his eyes so wide. But at Eneas's command, Tremelo lifted the woman's shoulders, and the two men carried her away from the edge of the cliff and back to the encampment.

Bailey grabbed Phi's hand. "Let's go," he said. Gwen scrambled behind Eneas and Tremelo to follow. Taleth ran next to them, and Bailey felt a radiating hope coming from her, mixed with intense worry. Whoever this tiger—this woman—was, Taleth loved her, and he wanted to find out why.

"Bailey," Tori said. She grabbed his wrist. Her face was crumpled, as if she was on the verge of crying. "You have to come see your dad. I think the bleeding is internal—"

Bailey didn't wait for her to finish. He ran back toward his dad, who was now leaning against Hal for support. "Dad!" Bailey called.

"Nice work back there," his dad said, his voice a raspy whisper. He clutched his side. Bailey moved his hand away and saw the blood had soaked through his shirt and jacket. There was a gaping wound. "It looks worse than it actually is," he joked.

"We need a doctor!" Bailey exclaimed, and threaded his arm under Herman's as if to lift him. But Herman moaned and Bailey pulled back, so as not to hurt him any further. "I'll run and get one right now."

"There's no time, Bailey," his dad said, doing his best to sit up. Hal helped him lean forward, and when he was secure in Bailey's arms, he moved to Tori's side to give him and his dad some room.

"Dad, I'm so sorry," Bailey said, his eyes welling with tears. "I got you into this. You wouldn't have fought if I hadn't—"

"If you hadn't been here," he said, touching his forehead to Bailey's, "then I wouldn't have had the opportunity to fight for the things I believe in. Fighting for your future made my life worthwhile."

"Dad, don't talk like that!" he whispered fiercely. "You still *have* a life ahead of you! We're going to patch you up. You'll get better. It's just a little blood." Though even as Bailey looked down he knew it wasn't a little blood—it was a lot of blood. His dad's skin was getting colder.

"I love you," he said, his eyes looking glassy. "Will you tell your mom I love her too?"

"You'll tell her yourself, Dad!"

But Bailey wasn't sure if he'd heard him or not. His dad's eyes were open but unfocused, like he was casually looking up at the sky. But he'd breathed his last breath, and Bailey clung to his body and cried.

Twenty~Six

TREMELO KNELT ON THE dirt inside the cool darkness of the tent. The woman lay on the table before him, and yet he almost did not believe that she was there. He knew her face so well that he was certain his memory was playing a strange and convincing trick on him, a trick that would soon end in baffled disappointment. He knew that face—but he had not seen it since he was nineteen years old.

"Elen," he whispered, although the woman was still asleep. "Is it you?"

The tent flap opened, letting in a triangle of moonlight. Eneas entered and held the flap open for the Tully, who carried a bowl of water and a jar of salve.

"I've sent Bailey and the others away," Eneas said. "She needs rest."

"Do you know her?" asked Tremelo. "Do you know who she was—I mean, who she is?"

Eneas smiled with pride.

"I am one of the few who knows that the Queen of the Underlands was not a tiger, but a human woman, one of the Velyn," said Eneas. "Elen saved the white tigers from massacre by leading them into the wilderness, in the only way she could. There, they waited until the kingdom needed them."

Tremelo brushed a piece of straw-colored hair away from Elen's sleeping face.

"She was always so brave," he said. "But that's not what I meant. Don't you know who she was to me? Isn't that why you brought me to her?"

Eneas looked puzzled.

"I brought you to her because you're the rightful ruler of Aldermere," he said.

Elen made a small moan of pain. Tremelo placed his hand over hers.

"She'll be very weak for a long time," said the Tully. "Weak in body, and weak in mind. She has been away from her own form for many years."

"Will she remember anything from before?" Tremelo asked. "Will she remember—?" He faltered. His own memories, which he had tried for so long to forget, were crowding his mind. He could hardly speak. He could remember everything.

"Do you know this woman?" asked Eneas.

Tremelo remembered a grove of thin, sparse evergreens, their needles shimmering after a mountain rainstorm. He remembered

Elen's hand in his, and the ring he'd placed on her finger. He'd hammered the silver himself.

My father's taking me back to the Gray City tomorrow, he'd said to her. *He says it's becoming too dangerous in the Peaks.*

You're never far away, she'd said. *I keep you in my heart, always.*

Nature bond us, they'd said together, *until Nature break us.*

Tremelo stood up to allow the Tully closer to the table. He placed his hand over his heart, which was beating so fast he felt he might either collapse, or lift into the air and fly.

"Who is she?" Eneas asked.

Tremelo smiled as it occurred to him that he had never before said what he was about to say—not even to his own father. Eneas would be the first human who would hear his secret, who would know what lived in his heart for twelve long years.

"She is my wife," he said.

Eneas stared at him, unspeaking. Then he looked down at Elen.

"Sir," he began, but faltered.

"We met as children," Tremelo said. "I loved her all my life. The Loon never knew. No one did. And when the Jackal—" He stopped. The memory of how he'd thought he'd lost her was still all too sharp. The news of the massacre had reached him and the Loon in the Gray City, and even then, he hadn't confessed just how much heartbreak it brought him.

Eneas stepped closer and lightly touched Tremelo's arm, drawing it away from Elen.

"My king, if this is true," Eneas began, "then there is something else you must know."

Twenty-Seven

BAILEY SAT BY HIS mother's side in the makeshift hospital, where the Tully tended to the wounded Allies and the Velyn sent out parties to gather the dead. And in the hours after his father died, his mother had remained stoic, though every so often she'd hug Bailey fiercely. "Your father loved you very much."

"He loved you too," he'd told her. "Those were his last words."

Bailey took breaks when the women of Defiance would visit and sit with his mom. During those moments, he'd stand in front of Eneas's tent waiting for any news of the mysterious woman. He wanted—needed—someone to survive when his dad could not.

To keep busy, he helped Tori and Hal gather fabric for bandages; he, Gwen, and Phi volunteered to forage for food. Doing something made him forget, for at least a little while, that he'd never hear his dad's laugh again. No more long-winded stories over porridge, or trips to the market with sacks full of grain.

It was not until the night had almost passed entirely, and the sun was about to rise, when Taleth perked her head up beside his bed and sauntered out of his tent. He rose and followed her. As she neared Eneas's tent, he felt her heartbeat quicken. She trembled, full of joy and relief. Outside the tent that had been the place of so much worry all night, there was Tremelo, standing tall with the woman beside him. Taleth padded straight up to her and lay down, her paws extended in front as her tail swished back and forth gracefully.

"Taleth," the woman whispered. "My brave friend."

Tremelo's eyes met Bailey's. They were shining, and his smile was almost sad—like something had shifted in him and he was puzzling how to put it back to right.

As he drew closer, Bailey studied the woman. She was very thin, but strong. She had wide swaths of freckles across her nose, cheeks, and shoulders. Her eyes, though—they were far from youthful. Her eyes were like deep wells of memory, wise but alert, and a little untrusting. And then Bailey remembered where he had seen this woman before.

"That's the woman from Taleth's memory," he said, the words catching in his mouth, breathless. And she was—her hair was the very same, though her face was slimmer and more careworn. She had the look of someone who had endured years of pain, pain that had only served to make her stronger.

"And my memories too," said Tremelo.

"Who is she?" Bailey asked, confused.

Tremelo took the woman's hand and led her to Bailey. Standing before him, she hesitated, then drew in a deep, strong breath. She looked to Tremelo as if she was unsure what to do or say.

"My name is Elen," she said finally. Then she cast her head downward and lifted her hands to her eyes. Bailey saw that she was hastily wiping away tears.

"You saved me," Bailey said. "You gave me to Taleth when I was just a baby."

The woman crouched. As she moved her hands away from her eyes and gazed at Bailey, a smile began to take shape on her lean, freckled face. She looked at him the way no one had ever looked at him before—with such love and happiness, but so much longing for something that had been lost, and might never return.

"Don't you know why?" she whispered. She reached out, but didn't touch him, not quite.

Bailey couldn't have predicted what he did next. It crept up and pounced on him, overpowering him before he could think of words: he burst into tears.

"I think—I think I do," he sputtered. "You're—you're my—" But he couldn't say the word. It carried too much hope to be said out loud.

Tremelo placed a hand on his shoulder. Bailey had almost forgotten that Tremelo was there.

"She's your mother, Bailey," Tremelo said. His voice trembled. Tremelo kept one hand on Bailey's shoulder, and with the other, he lightly touched the woman's face, as though he was afraid that she wasn't really standing there, and could disappear any moment.

"And that means," Tremelo continued, "that I am your father."

For a moment, Bailey was only aware of Taleth's joy as she circled them. She purred, and it seemed to echo off of the tree trunks. The sun was rising. The day was about to begin. Bailey looked from Elen to Tremelo, and then back again.

"We're a family?" he asked.

"We're a family," said his father.

Was it possible to have two families, and was it at all fair that he could feel twice as loved? But his heart seized; for a split second Bailey had forgotten his dad had died earlier on the battlefield. It was so unfair, to have to lose his father and gain another. He wanted both men, all of his family, joined as one. But that would never happen. And when he felt Tremelo's arms around him, he felt, too, that the True King shared the pain of this tragedy with him—and that they bore this great burden of losing fathers too soon together. Bailey felt safe for the first time in a great long while.

Epilogue

GWEN FELT A PLEASANT sense of déjà vu, roaming the halls of the newly restored palace. With each step, she experienced a different memory of her years growing up here with the Elder, each memory tinted with new happiness now that she'd returned, in the company of a new king. She nibbled at the raspberry tart she'd just commandeered from the kitchen as she rounded a corner and flitted down a stone staircase nearer the lower floors.

The owl Melem flew circles around the tower. Gwen paused at every other window to catch glimpses of her as she passed, and her heart soared. Someone soon she might perch at her window, or even eat from her hand. She hoped, at least. It might take time, she thought, but I'll heal.

Outside she could see Roger, Hal's uncle, instructing people and their kin in the business of planting a garden. The grass had shriveled up and the lawn fallen into disrepair during Viviana's occupation, but now they would make it beautiful again. From here, Gwen saw Hal hand Tori a bushel of flowers that he'd picked. In response, she leaned in and kissed him on the cheek; Hal turned so red Gwen could see his crimson cheeks from here. It made her smile.

Ahead, in an archway, a figure stood deep in thought.

"Emily?" Gwen asked the woman. "Mrs. Walker—are you lost?"

Emily Walker shook her head, chuckling to herself.

"I'm glad to see a familiar face—I'm afraid after all these weeks, I simply can't find my way through this maze! I was hoping to find Bailey."

"He's in the map room with Tremelo, I think," said Gwen. "I can show you the way." She wiped the crumbs from her hands and took Emily's arm.

They'd buried Emily's husband, Bailey's adoptive father, just a few days prior—in the woods next to the Elder. Both graves were covered in flowers, and Gwen felt certain they would always look like that—for years and years to come.

Together they walked back up the stairs and down a hall lined with carved archways and wooden beams. They stopped at a pair of tall doors carved with a mountain landscape. The room behind those doors was high ceilinged, with windows that overlooked the rooftops of the Gray City, and beyond, the first rolling hills that whispered of the distant presence of the Peaks.

Bailey leaned on his elbows on the central table, looking at a map nearly as large as the room itself. Next to him, Tremelo pointed at a spot illustrated in verdant green.

"What trouble are we plotting today?" asked Emily.

"Come and see," said Bailey. "Tremelo's taking me on a journey."

"Haven't had enough journeying yet?" asked Gwen. Bailey returned her smile.

"I never knew about the Underlands before Eneas showed them to me," said Tremelo. "The Loon had never spoken of them. And with Elen returning to her strength, she could guide us through them. Show us the parts of Aldermere that we need to protect the most."

"That does sound exciting," said Gwen.

"It's even better than that," said Bailey. "Elen was able to hide there because Aldermerians wouldn't come looking—and so everyone thought that the white tigers had gone extinct. Who knows what other kinds of animals could be hiding there? Creatures we'd thought had died long ago, or that we didn't even know existed."

"The Tully would be glad to hear that," said Gwen. "You'll have to write her if you find one."

Bailey smiled and looked again at the map.

"Look, Mom," he said. "This is where Elen is going to lead us, through the mountains here...."

"I wonder if I could ask you about something," Tremelo said to Gwen. He led her through the doors leading out onto a stone balcony. From here, the red and copper roofs of the Gray City spread out like scattered jewels all the way to the Fluvian. Gwen had missed being home. She'd nearly forgotten how lovely the city could be, especially under a loving ruler.

"You're no longer a student," Tremelo said. "Or an apprentice. So I have an official position for you."

"Oh?" said Gwen.

"The new Palace Seer," Tremelo said. "If you accept."

"Really?" said Gwen. "I'd be honored! It's just that . . ." She hesitated as she remembered the blind Seer Ama, tucked away in her mountain cave, far from the turmoil and the life of the kingdom. "I don't know if I can be a Seer in the same way that the old ones were. I don't think that I could just tell others what will or won't happen. I would want to help. I would wish to aid change."

"You can see a place for yourself in this kingdom's history, rather than a life outside of it," Tremelo said. "That makes you perfect for the job." Gwen pulled the Seers' Glass from her pocket and turned it over in her hands.

"You don't have to become like them," he said. "They watch what has yet to occur until all other sight erodes away. But you can see what the kingdom should be, and that is the kind of sight that comes from a good heart. We'll need you."

Gwen heard both footsteps and the faint sound of claws on the marble behind her. Elen, Bailey, and Taleth stood in the archway; Taleth stretched out her front paws and arched her back in the sun. Elen took Tremelo's arm and kissed his cheek.

"Are you ready?" Bailey asked Tremelo. "The rigi from Fairmount's due to come in any second. I told Phi we'd meet her at the platform. Shonfield couldn't chaperone—too busy with the rebuilding, I guess."

Tremelo smiled and clapped Gwen on the back.

"What do you think of my proposal?" he asked.

Gwen returned his smile.

"I accept," she said.

A familiar falcon swooped overhead. Gwen's heartbeat quickened.

"I think she might be early," she said. "Or Carin beat them here!"

"Come on, then!" said Bailey. He grabbed his mom's hand and pulled her out of the map room, with Tremelo and Elen following behind. Taleth pounced ahead as they hurried to the main hall of the palace, and then out into the cobblestone yard. Hal and Tori were already waiting, standing hand in hand. The rigi was just pulling in, its red, towering cars gleaming in the city sunlight. Gwen laughed as she ran. She thought she saw a hand waving from the second story of the front car, and she and Bailey waved back. Melem and Carin wove and dipped through the air, and Taleth's tail swished. Gwen's heart felt so full, that she wished the Elder could have been there to see her. He'd have been proud of her, of all of them. She and Bailey came to a stop, breathless, and waited for their best friend to emerge from the shining rigi into the sun.

Acknowledgments

ANIMAS WOULD BE NOTHING without the excellent team at Paper Lantern Lit: Lauren Oliver, Lexa Hillyer, Alexa Wejko, and Rhoda Belleza. I'm also grateful to Tara Sonin and PLL alums Angela Velez, Beth Scorzato and Adam Silvera for their vision at the start of the series and their support throughout. Thanks are due to agent Stephen Barbara and to the editorial team at Disney • Hyperion; Rotem Moscovich, Julie Moody, and Heather Crowley, steered this series into fruition with grace and keen insight. Thanks as always to my good friends and my family for their love and willingness to lend an ear. I'd especially like to thank my husband, to whom this series is dedicated.

Discover more
adventures in the
Animas series . . .

In a world where humans have
animal companions, one boy must
fulfil his hidden destiny.

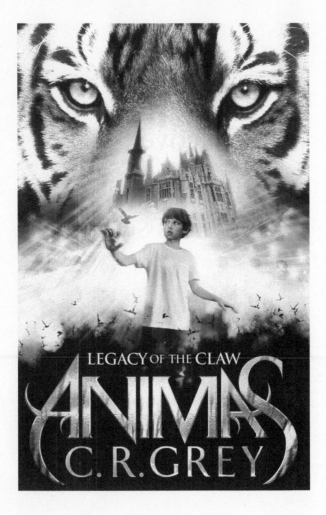

LEGACY OF THE CLAW

ANIMAS

C. R. GREY

When animals and humans unite,
amazing things can happen.

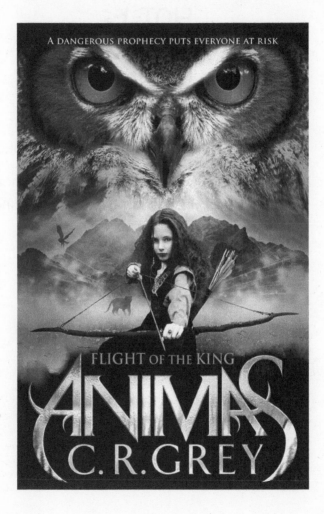

Thank you for choosing a Hot Key book.

If you want to know more about our authors
and what we publish, you can find us online.

You can start at our website

www.hotkeybooks.com

And you can also find us on:

We hope to see you soon!